Selfish

Part 1

CJ ALLEN

CJ ALLEN

Kings & Queens Publishing

15150 Preston Rd #300

Dallas, TX 75248

Selfish: Part 1

CJ Allen

Copyright © 2022 by CJ Allen

This novel is a work of fiction. Any resemblances to actual events, real people, living or dead, organizations, establishments or locales are products of the author's imagination. Other names, characters, places, and incidents are used fictitiously.

All rights reserved. No part of this book may be used or reproduced in any form or by any means electronic or mechanical, including photocopying, recording or by information storage and retrieval system, without the written permission from the publisher and writer.

Because of the dynamic nature of the Internet, and Web addresses or links contained in this book may have changed since publication and may no longer be valid. The views expressed in this work are solely those of the author and do not necessarily reflect the views of the publisher and the publisher hereby disclaims any responsibility for them.

Author's Note

This is CJ Allen, and I wanted to be the one to tell you what's up, so the story is straight, clear and true. I made the decision to change the name of my book from *Captain Save A Hoe* to *Selfish* due to a conflict of interest. This was done to avoid any legal issues that would arise from using that title. The main character's name was also changed from Christian to Blu'Jai due to another conflict of interest. This book has been revised, and bonus pages have been added in this rebooted installment. Oh yeah, *Part 2* is right around the corner.

Thanks for Your Support and Understanding,

CJ

ACKNOWLEDGEMENTS

Blu'Jai: Selfish?! Now wait a minute! CJ Allen, you couldn't come up with a better…I mean, *more appropriate* name for this book? SMH! I know you checked out the cover and he got me looking good as hell, so no problems there; but Blu'Jai Sky Ramos isn't a selfish bitch by a long shot. Over-zealous? Maybe. Selfish? No!

I know you're probably thinking, *why Blu'Jai over here being petty over a damn book title?* But I'm not being petty at all. You have the book in your hand, don't you? Shit, if I was really being petty, I wouldn't have let CJ write this shit. But my story is worth telling; it's kind of like a blueprint to teach folks how to win. See? From the go, I'm tryna give back. I ain't *selfish* at all! I know you're ready to get to the story, and probably sitting there like - *why the fuck is Blu'Jai even talking and this shit ain't even started?* Middle finger to you! Blu'Jai Ramos does what the fuck she wants, okay?

As a matter of fact, CJ... I'm going to do the acknowledgements. Just chill out for a minute! Ima give you the floor in just a bit! Damn! Impatient ass.

CJ: *Look, I've been working on these books for years. Been chasing this dream even through nightmares, so I'm just ready to take my spot in this literary game. But go ahead Blu'Jai. I ain't said shit!*

Blu'Jai: I know you haven't, but I'm looking at your face, CJ!

CJ: *Just don't be leaving folks out, cause I'm the one that has to hear that shit, not you! I don't want folks all in their feelings.*

Blu'Jai: Nah they need to stay out they feelings, cause ain't no money in there.

CJ: *Damn sho ain't! Just be sure you spell folks' names right and shit or Ima fuck yo ass up on the first page! Don't believe me, try me!*

Blu'Jai: CJ... I gotcha bruh!!! Ima make it quick so you can do your thing. You better be glad I love you or I wouldn't be letting you put my business all out there like this.

CJ: *I love you too Blu'Jai. Now hurry yo ass up!*

$ $ $ $ $

Blu'Jai: See... I told you! Blu'Jai Ramos gets whatever she wants. Let me thank these folks so y'all can see for yourselves. And if I forget your name and you did something to help with this book in any way, please don't tell CJ, because I think he's serious about fuckin me up on the first page. Just let *me* know and I gotcha on *Part 2*, because CJ will get on some ole bullshit with that damn pen!

First, we all are thanking God for His many blessings. I thank CJ's wife Tamara Allen for all the love and support she gives him; I see you cutting ya eyes over here at me, Tamara. CJ's like my big brother, so you ain't gotta watch me. Watch the money you guys make off this shit! Thank you to CJ's cousin Treva Perry over at Hair Addict, doing her best shit, lacing wigs and slaying edges. Dee "lilD" Porter, for coming through in the clutch and editing and fine-tuning this book. Thank you so much!

Wait a minute! Tell me this shit ain't happening! I deleted the list of names that I'm supposed to be thanking... *SHIT*!! Ima just say thank EVERYBODY! Oh wait; I have an idea! Ima just do it like this, but don't be a hater and go tell CJ:

Thank You to [Sign Your Name Here]:_____. CJ couldn't have done none of this without you!!! That should cover everything. Okay, enjoy my story. And if you spent your money on this book, thank you so much. If you just borrowed it from someone, stop being so damn cheap and support a brother that's trying to do something positive for a change.

CJ: *Blu'Jai! Now I'm an understanding man...*

Blu'Jai: Damn! Somebody already told on me. CJ, people just can't keep shit to themselves!

CJ: Well, I'm glad this was brought to my attention! I should've just done the shit myself because I almost let you close without thanking my mother!

Blu'Jai: Ummm! I'm SOOO sorry CJ! Ms. SHARON MARIE ALLEN, we all LOVE and miss you dearly!

That's the truth! Rest in Heaven, Mom! And a special thanks to my mother-in-law, who we just lost – Mary Elizabeth Roberson. Thank you for all your love, and I know my mother is excited to meet you! RIH Queen!

Always Remember…Never Give Up on Your Dreams!!!

SELFISH

'Sel-fish/ adj: concerned with one's own welfare excessively or without regard for others.

Prologue

Instead of begging for a seat, build your OWN TABLE...

Blu'Jai Ramos was 27 years old, and for the better part of those 27 years, she hadn't an inkling of an idea of her true purpose. She'd tried everything under the sun at least twice, and had even been a bit successful at some of her choices, but none of those things gave her the true fulfillment for which she yearned. Blu'Jai was always the most beautiful woman in any room she'd decide to step in. Her 5-foot frame, petite build, nice bubble butt, and honey golden skin was a work of art. Her brief stint at the gentlemen's club, Head Over Heels, where she graced the stages and entranced audiences with booty-shaking dances and sexy moves, is where she stacked the most bread. She could handle the visual ping-pong the men would play with her body from her chest to her love nest, but all the touching was enough to bring that career to an abrupt halt. However, there was some good to come out of that whole experience. Head Over Heels is where she'd met Kyron and her best friend Tazzell.

Blu'Jai didn't too much fuck with females because there was always some sort of underlying hate somewhere in the equation, but not with Tazzell. Tazz had her shit together, had a sense of direction, and businesses of her own, so she wasn't constantly all up in Blu's business. They hung out a lot together, mostly going to events like First Ladies: Style of Influence. That event gave them an inside peak at the role that First Ladies have played throughout the nation's history. Michelle Obama was a very inspiring woman to them both, and they felt that in order to be a leader, one would have to learn how to lead.

Kyron Preston was a major player in the streets. There had been droves of small-time ballers and street level hustlers in and out of Head Over Heels, but Kyron was a certified boss. Now, a lot of dudes *claim* to be bosses, but REAL BOSSES change people lives, and that's exactly what Kyron did for Blu'Jai. He moved her out of her one-bedroom apartment in Oak Cliff and into a two-bedroom high-rise in downtown Dallas off of Main Street. The skyline view from Blu'Jai's bay window was breathtaking, especially at night when the Dallas skyline was illuminated. Kyron was a clean cut, 6-foot-2 guy that was ruggedly handsome. He had the look of a company CEO: not too flashy with all the jewelry and extras of most hustlers, trying to show everyone that they have money. Kyron carried himself like a businessman and spoke intelligently at all times. He took care of Blu'Jai: rent, food, clothes and everything else her heart desired. He was truly a good man and always treated her with respect. That's why Blu'Jai couldn't understand why she hasn't been able to get Natural out of her mind.

Natural Faison was Blu'Jai's first and only love. They had been fucking around for over six years, but Natural had picked up a thirty-seven-month sentence in the Feds for scamming banks. Natural was well on his way to completely filling up his first safe when the Feds did a sting and nabbed him and his entire crew. She could still remember the phone call the day Natural went down.

"Blu'Jai, they got me." Natural sounded defeated.

"I saw it on TV," Blu'Jai said. "They are talking about you stole over half a million dollars from people's accounts and savings. They're painting a terrible picture of you, babe."

"Yeah I know." Natural admitted, nodding his head. "Look, I need you to go over to my place and clean up, ya feel me. I don't want these muthafuckas to be all in my shit. You know the code to get in, so go now."

Blu'Jai knew that Natural was talking about the safe. He needed her to get the money before the Feds did, so she threw on her Air Max tennis shoes and flew to his place. Within the next hour, Blu'Jai had more money in her possession than she'd ever had in her life. Just as she was pulling off, she saw the Feds pulling up. Luckily for Blu'Jai, they had just missed her by the skin of her teeth.

"Thank God!" she said aloud, smiling as she looked at the bag of money that sat in her passenger seat. She tossed on her shades, turned up Cardi B, and cruised coolly out of the neighborhood.

Blu'Jai immediately went shopping for new clothes, shoes and even splurged on a new pink Dodge Challenger. It wasn't as much money as she thought was in the safe, but it was well over two hundred thousand. She never made a habit of lying to Natural. He'd been so good to her over the years, but this money was her opportunity. It was her opportunity to do something with her life. Start a business or something. She was pretty good at doing hair, so maybe she would go to school to get her license and open a salon like her friend Latoya Logan.

"Bae, when I pulled up the Feds were already at your place, so I had to just keep driving and couldn't go in," Blu'Jai lied to Natural.

"Fuck!" he sighed. "I need a lawyer before these mufucka's drown me." He blew out a deep breath.

"You know all you have to do is give me the play and I'ma run it!" Blu'Jai tried to calm him.

"Don't worry about that, Ima pull some strings and get you one babe. I promise." Blu'Jai tried to ease the blow. Getting Natural a lawyer was the least she could do.

After Natural accepted a plea agreement for thirty-seven months, Blu'Jai put a couple thousand on his commissary and began making regular trips to visit once, sometimes twice a month. That was two and a half years ago. Natural was scheduled for release within the next 6 months.

Chapter 1

Be loyal behind my back!

Blu'Jai had been placed on pedestals behind velvet ropes since the day she'd met Kyron. His dizzying sex and irresistible smile were second to none, except for Natural of course. Last night Kyron had taken her, Tazzell and Tazzell's boyfriend Miles to a Brewing Arts Festival. It was an Urban Art Movement with more than 100 visual artists selling and commissioning original artworks. He and Miles both purchased several pieces, and they indulged in locally brewed adult beverages. They had dinner at Pera's Turkish Kitchen, a spot off Preston Road. Pera's Turkish Kitchen had lamb patties and thin-crusted Turkish pizza that were to die for.

Needless to say, it had been a wonderful night. Great company, excellent food, and plenty of laughs. Kyron had hung around for maybe an hour or so when they got back to Blu'Jai's place. He'd helped her hang two of the pieces he'd bought her from the art festival, then tossed back a couple shots of Paul Mason before he headed home. Blu was feeling a bit tipsy, so she told

Tazzell and Miles goodnight. After a quick shower, she felt like she was on cloud nine when she pulled her fluffy comforter up to her neck. Tazzell was in transition of finding a new place to live, so Blu being the friend she is, offered her extra room. It was only a temporary arrangement, but Blu enjoyed having Tazz around. Tazzell was 28 years old and had always treated Blu like a lil-sister, so Blu was glad to help.

Blu was sound asleep when her bedroom door flew open. "Blu!" Tazz screamed frantically. "Girl wake up!" Tazz snatched the covers off Blu.

"Is you fuckin' crazy!" Blu'Jai frowned. "This muthafucka better be on fire!"

"No, it's worse!" Tazz exclaimed, standing on the side of the bed in her t-shirt and panties. "I think Miles is Dead!"

"Miles!" Blu was wide awake now. "Dead? How is Miles dead and where was he at?"

"In my damn bedroom!"

"Tha fuck?" Blu looked confused. "Are you trying to tell me there's a dead man in *my house*?!" Blu pointed to herself.

"I mean… I really don't know what happened!" Tazzell tried to explain. "We were fucking, and the next thing I know Miles nutted then I felt his dead weight collapse on my back!"

"Bitch stop!" Blu laughed hysterically.

"No, I'm serious Blu! This shit aint funny! This nigga in here dead!"

"It's not funny." Blu tried to control her laughter. "Shit's just crazy!" She added. "So, Miles banging you from the back and the shit was so good he died in the pussy?" Blu laughed again.

"That's what the fuck happened!" Tazzell waved her hands in the air. "I normally put niggas to sleep, so I thought it was no big deal until I couldn't wake him up."

"Come on. Let's go in here and see." Blu said grabbing a pair of shorts and pulling them on.

"Yeah, because we got to find something to do with the body! I aint going to prison for fucking a nigga to death!" Tazzell said.

"Bitch I ain't in this shit! I'm just going to look! Nobody tell you to be up in here trying to live up to your old stage name, *Tazz Tha Azz*!" Blu said in a hushed tone.

They both tipped into the bedroom. A soft glow from the night lamp illuminated the room. Summer Walker could be heard singing at a low volume through the small, portable bluetooth speaker.

"See." Tazzell pointed to Miles laying on his back. "I told you he was dead."

"He is laying here all naked and shit. Damn." Blu'Jai gasped. "He looks like he breathing to me."

"Nah Blu'Jai, I just checked his pulse and didn't feel shit."

"Check that shit again! I'm telling you it looks like he is breathing! Turn on the damn lights so we can see! Shit!"

Tazzell flipped on the lights then walked over and put two fingers on the left side of Miles neck.

"Bitch you touching the wrong side!" Blu'Jai shouted. "If this nigga ain't breathing, you better find a way to get him in your car or I'm calling 911, 'cause this some bullshit right here."

"You can feel a pulse on both sides, with your illiterate ass!" Tazzell flipped her off.

"Nah fuck YOU, and this nigga! Both of y'all got to go! I ain't got time fa no shit like this!"

"Are you serious?" Tazzell whined. "You gone just throw me out and threaten to call the police on me when you know I aint did shit?"

"Tazz you should've been called the laws!"

"Bitch I have a warrant!" Tazzell cried.

"So, you don't call for help because you have a raggedy ass warrant?" Blu'Jai shook her head.

"I didn't know what to do! I'm scared shitless Blu!" Tazzell began to sob.

Blu'Jai hugged Tazzell tight and felt the tremble in her body. "We have to call the police Tazzell. You just tell the truth and explain what happened. I don't think they can charge you with anything."

"Yeah, you're right. I'll call them. I should've called them at first. I'm sorry."

"You good. But before you call, let's check his pockets and get his money. No sense in letting the police get it." Blu'Jai suggested.

"Touch my money I'll fuck you up." Miles said in a groggy voice, scaring the fuck out of them both.

$ $ $ $ $

"Yes, I'm here to see Natural Faison." Blu'Jai informed the correctional officer.

"His inmate numbers?" the officer asked.

"2286693." Blu'Jai rattled off while zipping her thigh high heel boots back up.

She would swear that some of the females that pat and searched the visitors enjoyed touching and rubbing her body. Most of the time it was more of a sensual caress than a pat search.

"Table 2." The officer pointed, then picked up the phone to call for Natural.

Blu'Jai strolled to the vending machines and all eyes were on her. Dudes watched her smooth sashay as her heels *click clacked* across the tile floor. Women's faces were twisted to hell as they watched their husbands and boyfriends get mesmerized by Blu'Jai's presence. Blu'Jai had practically painted on her jeans, and her long, curly hair would put one in the mind of Dani Leigh. After grabbing a few snacks and a couple of green teas, she found her table and waited.

Natural stepped into the visitation room looking good as hell. Blu'Jai licked her lips at the sight of his 6-foot-2, chocolate-covered frame and stood up to give him a hug. Natural sported a fresh pair of Forces, and his uniform was immaculately pressed. His smile lit up the room, and his well-toned body garnered the same type of attention from the women as Blu'Jai had done with the men.

"How are you?" Natural asked after a long, warm hug and a passionate kiss. He slapped her on the ass and took his seat.

"Had to put Tazzell out the other day." Blu'Jai said, popping a chip into her mouth.

"Why?" Natural twisted the top off both bottles of Green Tea.

"Too much drama." She shook her head, picking an onion off of one of the deli sandwiches she'd bought.

"That's probably God continuing to work his magic, so don't be fucked up about it."

"I ain't fucked up. Tazz is my girl, but I can't be around a lot of bullshit. You know what I'm saying?"

"I feel ya." Natural nodded and took a bite of his sandwich. "I have some good news though. I wanted to tell you face to face, that's why I didn't say nothing when I called Friday."

"What?!" Blu'Jai stopped mid chew.

"I'll be home next week," Natural smiled and grabbed Blu'Jai's hand.

"That's wonderful babe!" she screamed. "Ima start getting shit ready as soon as I get back!"

Natural held out his hand and Blu'Jai held it in hers.

$ $ $ $ $

"Hey Kyron!" Blu'Jai called him as soon as her visit was over. "I'm just leaving Seagoville. I told you I was going to go and visit my brother today."

"Yes, I do recall you mentioning that. So, how's he doing?" Kyron asked concerned.

"Good news, he just told me that he'd be home next week! I'm so excited!"

"That's fantastic!" Kyron smiled. "I can't wait to meet him."

"I can't either. He'll be staying with me for a while until he gets on his feet."

"Oh ok. Well you know I'll help in any way I can. I have a few cars sitting. I'll take him over to have a look whenever he's ready. You know, something to get around in until he readjusts."

"You'd do that?" Blu'Jai couldn't believe Kyron's generosity.

"I'm sure your brother is a good man. Just have him give me a call when he gets settled."

"I will and thank you so much Kyron."

"No problem. I have an important call coming in, so I need to let you go."

"Handle your business."

"Been a pleasure." Kyron smiled.

"Same here." Blu'Jai ended the call.

Thirty minutes later Blu'Jai pulled into the parking lot of Latoya-Logan's Salon. She snatched her sunglasses off her face as soon as she walked through the door.

"Look at her, just smiling and shit!" a woman that was lounging in a chair waiting to be shampooed said. "I know she ready fa Natural to get home!" the woman laughed.

"Yeah, I'm glad to hear he's coming home too!" Latoya Logan added as she rinsed color from the head of one of her clients.

"I just found out myself not even an hour ago, so I'm wondering how Dallas, Texas already knows!" Blu'Jai said.

"Girl it's all over Instagram!" Latoya laughed.

"Oh really." Blu'Jai raised a brow. "Well yeah, he'll be home next week." she confirmed, grabbing a seat.

"So, does this mean Kyron Preston becomes eligible?" a thick, chocolate sista asked with a smirk.

"Eligible for what?" Blu'Jai shot back. "He already has enough raggedy ass hoes trying to be in his face, he doesn't need no more."

Tameca rolled her eyes. "Yeah…but I figured since Natural getting out Kyron would be losing a raggedy hoe and there may be room for a classy chick to get the dick."

"Hey, hey!!" Latoya pointed her rattail comb in the direction of both ladies. "Knock that shit off up in here! Act like you been somewhere! We don't do hood rats up in here!" Latoya preached.

"Bitch ain't got no business in my shit anyway." Blu'Jai mumbled.

"Bitch what you say?!" Chocolate spat.

"I'm not going to ask you two again!" Latoya injected.

"Any more of that BS Ima have to ask you both to leave."

Blu'Jai snatched up her handbag and headed for the door.

"Latoya I'm sorry. I have a lot on my mind, so I'll just reschedule."

"That's fine. You be blessed girl." Latoya smiled.

"You too." Blu'Jai pushed the door open then turned around and gave Chocolate an evil eye. "Oh, and umm… Kyron don't fuck with fat bitches, so you may want to lose 50-60lbs before you even look his way." Blu'Jai said with a laugh.

Chapter 2

The biggest communication problem is we do not listen to understand. We listen to reply.

Blu'Jai's gleaming white Lexus was parked outside of the prison early Friday morning waiting for Natural to emerge from the bottomless pit of the living dead. Kyron had just given her the car a few weeks prior as a gift, so the new smell of leather was still able to overpower Blu's YSL perfume. She checked her appearance in the rearview mirror for the umpteenth time and pulled out her lip gloss to apply another thick coat, when she heard two soft taps on the window. A smile plastered her face as she jumped out the car and into Natural's arms.

"Heeeyyy!!!" Blu'Jai screamed. "Welcome home!" she sang as Natural picked her up by her butt cheeks.

"What's good baby?" Natural asked coolly.

"You." Blu'Jai kissed him passionately. "Jump in and let's get outta here!!!"

"Nice whip!" Natural complimented, throwing his bag in the back seat.

"Yeah, it was a gift."

"A gift?" Natural looked at Blu'Jai suspiciously.

"Don't look at me like that! I wanted to wait til' you got out to talk to you about all of this!" Blu'Jai waved her hand.

"All what?" Natural gave Blu'Jai a hard stare.

"I met a guy named Kyron Preston a couple years ago when I danced over at Head Over Heels," she said as she navigated the new coup through traffic.

Natural sat quietly and listened. Being quicker to listen versus talking was something he had to learn in his thirty-month prison stay.

"Well Kyron has been taking care of me. The address you've been writing to off Main is the apartment that he pays for. He bought me this car and even told me he'd help *you* get on your feet."

"Help me?" Natural looked disgusted.

"Yeah baby," he knows all about you. He knows that you'll be staying with me and he's planning on giving you a car too. He wants to meet you. He's a real boss type nigga and I think it would be crazy not to at least meet the man."

"And you saying this yo nigga, but he knows all about me?" Natural asked in disbelief.

"No… you're my nigga! He's just a nigga I fuck with, and yeah he knows about you! But I told him you were my brother though."

$$$$$

Blu'Jai was full of shit and surprises. As they cruised back to her penthouse, she and Natural both rode silently, each collectively in their own thoughts. Natural, trying to soak in his freedom as well as the pending situation. Blu was thinking back to how she would always win, and she would always win at any cost. She prided herself on it. Just like when Kyron made his first visit to her apartment when she was staying in South Oak Cliff. Her mother, Melanie, was staying over for a week, sleeping on the couch. There had been problems over at her place, Belmont Village Senior Living. Two elderly women had wandered off in a month's time, so Blu'Jai brought her mom to her home until the facility could straighten their shit out. Kyron was knocking at the door and Blu'Jai welcomed him in, introducing her mother.

"Kyron Preston, this is my mom Melanie Ramos."

"Pleased to meet you ma'am!" he gave a warm smile and shook her hand."

Blu'Jai had prepared lamb burgers, potato wedges and milkshakes. They kicked back and watched Tyler Perry movies while enjoying each other's company. By the time Kyron was preparing to leave, he suggested that Blu'Jai find a place for Melanie because she was too sweet and old not to be comfortable in her own space.

"Your couch is no place for Ms. Ramos." Kyron told Blu'Jai.

Unbeknownst to Kyron, Blu'Jai spent the entire time lying about her mom's financial situation, and Kyron fell right into her trap. He began paying for the place at the Belmont Village that Melanie was already occupying. Not long after that small paycheck from Kyron started coming in, he moved Blu'Jai into her downtown High rise.

I'm a bad bitch, she thought to herself, then peered over at Natural.

$ $ $ $ $

Natural took in the sights of the city and how much it had changed in only three years. What was only a light sprinkle when Natural took his first step outside of those prison walls, was now a pouring rain. The faint sound of Blu'Jai's windshield wipers along with Chris Brown's "Sex You Back to Sleep" was the only sound in the car. Natural bobbed his head and finally broke the tension.

"So, you told this dude I'm your brother huh?" he asked as he continued to stare out the window.

"Yeah. I mean, what was I supposed to tell 'em, Natural? I feel like this is a good opportunity for both of us. It's your first day out, don't waste it in your feelings over dumb shit."

Natural turned his gaze to Blu'Jai then turned the music up.

Don't say a word no, girl don't you talk

Just hold on tight to me girl

Sex you back to sleep girl

Natural flashed a devilish smile and rubbed Blu'Jai's thigh, "My girl." he smirked.

$ $ $ $ $

Blu'Jai dug two keys out of her black leather, metal studded titty-hugging jacket and handed one to Natural.

"This is your key." she eyed Natural, standing back on her bowed legs looking like a fuckin' sex goddess in her ripped stretch skinny jeans.

Natural stared at his girl for a minute before inserting the key. Blu'Jai licked her lips like they were Natural's.

"Surprise!!!" everyone screamed as he pushed the door open.

"WELCOME HOME!!!" they sang as Natural walked in. Miles was the first to greet Natural with a warm brotherly hug, followed by Tazzell.

"Sup girl!" Natural smiled.

"You boy!" Tazz cheered kissing his cheek.

Natural looked around at the light decorations and food. The gesture was heartwarming to say the least. He grabbed Blu'Jai, about to kiss her for being so thoughtful, when she placed her palm flat on his chest to quickly halt him.

"Natural this is Kyron - the one I was telling you about!" Blu'Jai gave a fake smile pointing to the direction Kyron was standing with a glass of Hennessy Black in hand.

Natural's bad boy gaze casually followed Blu'Jai's finger. He tried to keep his attitude in check as he reached for Kyron's hand.

"Good to finally meet you bruh!" Kyron flashed a debonair smile." "Heard nothing but great things about you!"

Blu'Jai's stomach muscles tightened. Natural's aura got under her skin and warmed her body like a quick shot of patron.

"Pleasure to meet you as well." Natural replied. Humor edged his voice and played down her spine.

Kyron had on a Fenix Italian cream colored button-up dress shirt with his sleeves rolled up and three buttons unfastened. His dark brown slacks and genuine ostrich shoes reeked money. Kyron stepped over and slipped an arm around Blu'Jai's waist. Tazzell had to fight to keep from laughing at the whole damn scene. She'd told Blu that the whole coming home party wasn't a good idea, especially inviting Kyron, but Blu was afraid to be alone with

Natural. She figured the party would give him time to cool off after she broke the news, and so far, it was working. It was only five of them at the apartment, but for Blu'Jai that was plenty.

"Um, sis can I see you in the backroom for a minute?" Natural asked. "I'd really like a quick shower and a change of clothes before we get this shit started."

"Very understandable!" Kyron said. "I had Blu'Jai grab you a few clothes, but I didn't really know your style, so we can hook up tomorrow and get some things more of your taste."

"I appreciate that." Natural nodded. "Blu," Natural gave her a tight eyed look.

"I'm about to turn some music on!" Tazzell said, giving Natural a warning brow. Tazzell tossed him a 'don't be back there on no bullshit' look. He returned her look with a smirk of his own.

Blu'Jai wasn't really worried as she led Natural to the back room. He'd never been an abusive man, and with guests present she was sure he wouldn't do much more than vent. As soon as they stepped into the bedroom Natural closed the door behind them.

"Please don't start," Blu'Jai huffed.

"You think this is how I wanted to spend my first day out?!" Natural spat between gritted teeth. "HUH?!!!"

"I just..."

"You just what?" he cut her off. "You just a selfish ass bitch! Gotta have every muthafuckan thing! Always on some bullshit! You always have been a selfish bitch. Always have and always will be!"

"Natural!" Blu'Jai whined.

"Bitch get me a towel and some boxers!" he demanded as he headed into the bathroom and stripped out of his clothes. Natural turned on the shower disgusted.

"Here." Blu'Jai mumbled as she sat a towel and a pair of Ethicka boxers on the sink countertop.

Blu'Jai couldn't help but admire Natural's strong back and muscular ass cheeks. When he turned around to thank her, Blu'Jai eyes were glued to his husky chest, slowly making their way down to his sculpted abs. Those prison khakis had done this man no justice. She tried to resist, but her eyes seemed to have a mind of their own. She tried to turn away and get the hell out of the bathroom but couldn't stop her eyes from finding his dick. '

Damn! she said to herself. There it was…thick…black and long. Just hanging in all its splendor.

Natural snatched the shower curtain open and frowned at her. She could've sworn that he shook his dick at her as he climbed in and snatched the curtain closed. Blu'Jai sucked her teeth and stomped back into the room. Seconds later she came back into the bathroom butt ass naked. Natural could see her flawless body through the clear shower curtain but was unmoved as he continued to soap up his body. She closed the lid on the toilet and sat down. She put her left foot on the edge of the tub and held the other up so high that her thigh rested on the front of her shoulder. She squeezed her nipple with one hand and spread her pussy lips apart with the other. Pinching her nipple and playing with her clit, Blu'Jai watched as Natural's long soapy dick slowly start to stand at attention. His eye's locked in on her Brazilian waxed pussy. Her eyes on his African artwork. Natural gripped the base of his dick and began to stroke its length; both unable to take their eyes off the exquisite sexual drama that was being played out. Natural went into a zone and started jacking his dick off with speed and force, while Blu'Jai added a second finger into her dripping wet pussy. His dick pulsed once and made his toes ball up.

"Bitch" he suddenly mouthed as a load of nut shot all over the curtain suddenly.

Thick cum painted the plastic, cascading down when Blu'Jai became tense and started convulsing madly as an orgasm shuddered through her body.

"AHHHHSSSSHHHIIIITTTT!!!" she sang as her eyes rolled into the back of her head.

Natural suddenly snatched the curtain open and yanked Blu'Jai up from the toilet forcefully. He spun her around and bent her over the sink.

"Bitch you want to play?" he growled, slapping his semi hard dick across her thick ass cheeks repeatedly. "Ima show your ass how to play!" he spat, lifting one of her thighs on the countertop.

Natural pushed his dick inside of Blu's warm pussy and fucked her roughly from behind.

"Selfish ass bitch! Got a nigga in the front and another in the back!" he pounded, grabbing a hand full of hair.

"Naaaturaaalll!" she wined. "Baby, slow down!"

"Shut up and take this dick bitch!"

He slapped her ass cheek and watched it jiggle. He fucked her so hard he tried to knock her head through the mirror. Natural felt his nut tingling again. The pounding sound his forceful thrust was making against Blu'Jai's ass cheeks was intoxicating. He pounded repeatedly until she screamed for God. He stopped and gave her three final pumps!

ONE...

"Natural!" she screamed his name.

TWO...

"FUUUUUCK!" she cried.

THREE... He pumped.

"Ummmmmm!!!" she tapped on the countertop repeatedly as Natural pulled out and nutted on her ass.

CJ ALLEN

Chapter 3

When you have a million-dollar vision, don't hang around one-cent minds.

"We thought y'all had gotten lost back there!" Tazzell shot Blu'Jai a knowing look.

"Nah, big bruh and I got caught up discussing some family issues," Blu'Jai replied rolling her eyes at her friend.

"Come here baby." Kyron said to Blu'Jai with a smile.

Blu'Jai strutted over to Kyron who was sitting on a bar stool at the island. She got nervous as fuck when he pulled her between his legs and kissed her forehead.

"I made a couple of calls and I was thinking that it wouldn't be a bad look to offer your brother a position so he can make his own money. You know what I'm saying? That's if he's interested," Kyron said in a hushed tone.

"Well, that's something you would have to get with him on, Kyron. I mean, he just got out so he may kind of want to ease back into things, ya know."

"Well, he's a big man. He can make his own choices; I just wanted to run it by you before I got with him."

"That's fine. Thank you, baby," Blu'Jai nodded just as Kyron kissed her lips and smacked her behind.

Natural took in the whole scene as he took a few swallows of a Corona." I need a partner on these dominoes, Kyron. You play?"

"I painted the dots on them shits!" Kyron laughed, pulling up a seat at the table.

Natural and Kyron beat Miles and Tazzell like they stole something. After a couple more beers and a few good laughs, Natural was finally able to loosen up a little. Blu'Jai had cooked a seafood gumbo that included chicken breasts, shrimp, crabmeat, okra, tomatoes and onions. Shit smelled good as hell. Blu'Jai fixed Kyron's plate while Tazzell fixed Miles and Natural's meals. Kyron blessed the food and they all dug in. The meal was just as delicious as it smelled.

After everyone was good and full, Blu'Jai and Tazzell went into cleanup mode while the men chilled out on the balcony and puffed cigars. Natural realized that Kyron wasn't a bad dude at all. The two had discussed a business proposal, and although Natural had never fucked around in that line of work, the type of numbers Kyron tossed around definitely snatched his attention. The two had made plans to hook up early the next morning, and Natural was looking forward to it.

$ $ $ $ $

At 6 am Natural was already on his last set of push-ups. Kyron was supposed to be there by seven, so Natural had plenty of time to give his bald head a fresh shave and get a good shower. Ten minutes till seven and Kyron was calling Natural's phone.

"Hello?" Natural answered the iPhone Blu'Jai had gotten him.

"I'm about a block away, so you can come down if you're ready." Kyron said.

"I'm already standing out here." Natural replied as he saw a white Bentley Coup pulling up on him.

Kyron smiled as Natural reached for the door. "I like that shit. Beat *me* to the muthafuckan spot!" Kyron nodded his approval. "You operate like *I* operate. Muthafucka tell me to meet 'em at seven-thirty, I'm there at seven! Shows that you respect time. Shows character. *That's* what the fuck I'm talking about." Kyron pulled off. "Breakfast on me!" he said, shaking Natural's hand, then pulling the luxury vehicle smoothly back into traffic.

He turned the music up as they floated through the streets of downtown Dallas. Kyron bobbed his head and sang along with, "I ain't ask no nigga fa nothing. I took the harder way."

Natural grinned and peered out the window as they passed some beautifully designed buildings. He heard Kyron loud and clear. He understood the language he was speaking through the music. He'd taken the harder way. No handouts. No begging.

They headed to the Yolk, a hot spot over in One Arts Plaza. They cruised through Deep Ellum, then made a right on Lamar Street.

"This a nice whip.'" Natural complimented, enjoying the comfort of the plush leather he was reclining on.

"Appreciate it man. Fruits of plenty of long days and nights of labor." Kyron said as he whipped into a parking space.

$ $ $ $ $

Kyron ordered the Belgian waffles topped with strawberries and whipped cream along with scrambled eggs, turkey bacon and orange juice. Natural had an order of egg whites, hash browns, buttermilk biscuits with white gravy, sausage, and Welch's grape juice.

"So, your sister says that you're pretty good with numbers?" Kyron said as he poured maple syrup over his waffles.

Natural shook his head in disbelief. Blu'Jai is 50 shades of fucked up he thought to himself. "I guess I'm okay." he answered, stuffing some of the fluffy eggs into his mouth.

"When Blu'Jai told me how you lost all your earnings and basically had to start over, I was inclined to meet you. Hell, how can a man remain sane when a muthafucka empties his bank account and locks him away? That is enough to make a brother lose a few marbles out of his sack." Kyron said. "I've had the opportunity to look at my failures in the face for a while. Been falling forward for a long time. So now I'm tryna clean up my side of the street by offering you a Golden Ticket."

"Well I think it's only fair to tell you who I'm not, before I tell you who I am," Natural interjected.

"Listening."

"Not a dealer, but definitely a bonified hustler."

Kyron smiled. "I gathered that from your sister, and that's why I want you to manage and operate my new coffee shop. It's called Kyron's Cup."

"Really?"

"Yeah man! I think you will be great! What, you thought I was trying to put a brick in your hand?" Kyron laughed.

"The thought crossed my mind. I mean Blu'Jai did tell me you were heavy in the streets."

"Well actually, I've never really been in the 'streets.'" Kyron made air quotes with his fingers. "I actually started off as a cop."

"A cop?" Natural looked surprised.

"Dallas PD. Was an undercover narcotics agent." Kyron peered at Natural. "So, my unit had surveillance on Sampson Richard."

"Sam Rich!" Natural nodded. "He had the streets on lock back in the day!"

"Same guy." Kyron said. "So, one night I was tailing Sampson and was fortunate enough to witness his murder."

"He got killed in his front yard," Natural recalled the incident.

"Correct. So, I made a decision that forever changed my life. Instead of me calling the murder right in or going after the suspect, I recovered the keys to his estate and searched it for hours. I was able to find two million dollars. Although I locked the house back up and placed the keys back where I found them in the grass, surveillance cameras were able to catch me removing the large trash bag from the house. The agency suspected it was money but couldn't prove it. So, I was forced into a quiet resignation- which was fine with me. Hell, I became a millionaire over night; and the department wouldn't have done shit but find a way to keep the shit themselves, had they found it. So, I have what I call 'Fuck You' money; but 'Fuck You' money requires a huge amount of discipline. The minute you go a penny over, then you lose your freedom again. See, I made that decision because I had money problems; and if money is the cause of your worries, then you must restructure your life. I had all the info on the dealers in the city, so I invested a few hundred thousand here and there. Now here I sit. A made man. One thing I've learned is, if you give a muthafucka enough power to feed you, you also give him enough power to starve you. Now my hands are completely clean, but most people think I still hustle like that. Even your sister."

"So, your plan is-"

"My plan is to allow you an opportunity to feed yourself." Kyron cut him off.

"Where is the shop you're building?"

"Finish up and I'll show you. It's practically finished. Its off Main street near El Centro College. We'll go check out the property, then get you a car to get around in."

Natural and Kyron instantly clicked. They hung out the rest of the day. They went clothes shopping, and Kyron even tossed Natural a set of keys to his sporty Jeep wrangler. The two toured his coffee shop and Kyron took carefully detailed notes to ensure the success of the new establishment.

The following day, Kyron began placing orders for different coffee blends. Everything from the exotic earth blends, which was a roasted blend of Indonesian and South American beans, to the White-Knuckle Blend, which was a blend of Robust and Arabia beans. The target grand opening was merely a week away, and there was still a lot of work to do in only a short time.

$ $ $ $ $

"So, you really serious about all this coffee shop shit?" Blu'Jai frowned as she stood with her hands on her hips while Natural pecked away at a laptop at the kitchen table.

"Why wouldn't I be?" Natural returned her disgusted look.

"One!" she held up a finger. "Ain't no money in no shit like that! Two, you ain't never been no damn worker. And three, we supposed to be playing this nigga, not getting all friendly!"

"How the fuck you think I'm getting friendly?" Natural questioned.

"I hear yo silly ass all up in here giggling and grinning! Friendly ass!"

"Fuck out of my face Blu!" He continued tapping away on the laptop.

"If you wanted to start a business you should have told me that! I fuck with *bosses*, not the *help*!" Blu'Jai pierced.

"And where the fuck was you gone get the type of capital required to fund a business?" Natural chuckled.

"I have some money nigga! I ain't never been a broke bitch!" Blu'Jai stated. "I've been grinding, and I own some fuckin' stocks in Amazon! You better get yo fuckin' facts straight nigga. I've been doing my best shit!"

"How much stock do you have in Amazon?" Natural questioned.

"Enough to keep me dry on a rainy day," Blu'Jai smirked.

Chapter 4

Entrepreneurship is living a few years of your life like most people won't, so that you can spend the rest of your life like most people can't.

Natural and Kyron were basically inseparable. They could be spotted together day or night, like they had known each other all their lives. They worked hard to get Kyron's Cup up and running, and Kyron felt comfortable enough to share things with Natural that he had never shared with anyone else - like him being an ex-cop and how he'd gotten his money. Kyron told Natural how he had bought a few homes around the city and was renting them out. It felt like they were long lost brothers. Natural told Kyron how he really wasn't a gangster type dude. In fact, he'd been his high school valedictorian. He was a fuckin' brainiac. A master problem solver - and now his hope was to apply his brain power to Kyron's Cup.

"So, the grand opening is tomorrow." Natural stated as he sipped on Jack Daniels Honey with Kyron at his estate in Cedar Hill, a suburb about 20 minutes south of Dallas.

"Finally!" Kyron smiled as he dropped a few cubes of ice in his glass as he stood at the mini bar.

"Yeah…" Natural stretched his words. "Big bro, I want to shoot straight with you about something."

"Fire," Kyron poured himself a shot of Jack.

"Blu isn't my sister. I've been fucking with her for years." Natural admitted. "I see big things ahead of us, and I don't want no dumb shit like this to fuck it all up. Plus, real niggas are hard to find out here man. I just don't want you looking at me like I carry mine all foul."

Kyron nodded. He stared at Natural a minute. Natural couldn't read his expression. Kyron took a big swallow from his glass then stuck his free hand into the pocket of his slacks.

"I'm glad you told me that before we got too deep in our business endeavors!" Kyron said "Now I truly feel like I can trust you. I've always known who you were. I'm an ex-cop bruh. Shit, I was on you for a minute there, until the Feds took over that investigation."

"So, you knew." Natural looked shocked.

"From day one. But I respect your mind, and I know we can do some great shit together. If you want your girl, I'm out ya way." Kyron promised. "To get more out of life you have to get more out of yourself."

"Nah man. I'm just hanging around until I get back on my feet, so do you." Natural said.

$ $ $ $ $

"So, I'm like 'I fuck with *boss* dudes, not no damn *workers*.' He could've just come to me, and I would've put the money up to get our own shit off the ground!" Blu'Jai said to Tazzell as she carefully swooped her baby hairs into her hairline. The two had been on FaceTime for the last twenty minutes.

"Well why didn't you just give the man his money back anyway. I mean, it was rightfully his to begin with." Tazzell frowned. "You stole Natural's money, then want to sit up here and talk shit like he the one who's fucked up."

"Invested, bitch! Not 'stole!'" Blu'Jai corrected. "And I earned that money anyway, because if I recall correctly it was *my* ass on the line when I was up in his spot opening that safe! Not his!" Blu'Jai worked her neck. "Ya ass sounding a little salty over there, checking fa my dude's wallet. What's really going on?" she asked with accusing eyes.

"Just calling you on yo shit! Fuck you mean what's really going on?" Tazzell challenged.

"I'm just saying you sounding really suspect right now. Like a lightweight hater."

"What the fuck ever Blu. When you wrong you wrong!"

"And when you broke you broke!" Blu'Jai popped back.

"I'm a real bitch. And when you real, real shit happens for you." Tazzell said in a cocky tone. "Just like when you closed your door on me, God opened another. That's why I called you before we got sidetracked. I wanted to tell you thank you. When you put me out, I was pissed! I had nowhere to go-"

"Tazz don't come for me on that pity shit! I knew you could take yo ass right on over to Miles! Shit, you gone hold it against me because I don't want that type of bull crap up in my spot. On top of the fact that my man just got home!"

"*Yo man?*" Tazzell laughed. "Blu, you don't give a fuck about no one but yourself."

"Get out ya feelings, 'cause ain't no money in there."

"Whatever!" Tazzell smacked. "I'm good! *Real good!*"

"Well good! I gotta get off this phone and get ready for the grand opening."

$ $ $ $ $

Blu'Jai's white linen, strapless jumpsuit hugged her model-like frame like it was tailored by Gucci himself. The deep V-Neck and open arms highlighted her perfect cleavage and flat tummy. She slipped on a pair of gold mules, double checked her hair, make up, and of course she looked flawless!

Check, check, and check me the fuck out! she said to herself smiling, extremely pleased with what she saw. Blu'Jai blew herself a kiss then grabbed the keys to her Lexus.

The day had turned out to be beautiful, despite the weather report. They say it was supposed to be a 70% chance of rain, but it wasn't a cloud in the sky. Blu turned up her radio and threw on some shades as she floated through uptown. She was pumping R. Kelly's classic *'Bump n Grind Remix'* to the max. All that talk about not listening to Kells because he was in trouble on pervert charges didn't faze her one bit. She loved her some R. Kelly music and could care less about his personal life. Guilty or not the nigga cold SANG, and that's how she saw it. Hell. She was a freak her damn self and was thinking that the pied piper could've just hit her up and she would've matched his inner freak. She wasn't even tripping on his fetish to pee on folk. Shit, Blu'Jai wanted to piss on his ass too!

She rocked in her seat and snapped her fingers to the beat as she sang along with Kells. *'I got what you want, you got what I need, homie lover friend is all I want to be, it's that pretty brown round driving me wild ooohhh child, things about to get a little freakier...* She looked over at a Spanish guy that was admiring her karaoke-like performance, sitting in a Maserati at the light next to her and sang. *"I will have you singing like a Mockingbird wooorrrd..."* She blew him a kiss flirtatiously and he blushed with a wink and a light chuckle before she zipped away through the green light. Mr. Maserati was handsome, and normally she would've been ready to eat his ass alive - but she already had a lot on her plate, so there was really no room for an appetizer. She was all about dinner and dessert.

As she pulled into the parking lot of Kyron's Cup, she was immediately impressed with all the high-end cars that littered the parking area. *Maybe Natural was on to something,* she thought, as she checked her appearance one last time.

The boy really is smart as fuck, she said to herself. *Knowing him, he's already figured out a way to transfer all the money to a private account! Damn! That's it! Shit, I'm the slow one*! she laughed at her own realization. *'He's been scheming this whole fucking time and here I am doubting his G!'*

Natural has always been on his shit; how could she have ever thought that he would settle for being a worker? She should've figured it was more to the shit.

Blu'Jai's walk was a little lighter as she made her way through the parking lot. She felt so much better about the situation now that she had figured it out. As she made her way to the door, she noticed something that she hadn't noticed when she first arrived. She paused and took in the sign that graced the store front: Kyron's Cup, Blends All Natural. Blu'Jai smiled. *All* Natural *huh?* she giggled to herself. She was tickled as hell about the way she had been able to put all the pieces together. Natural had a bigger hand in this coffee shop than just pouring some motherfuckin' hot water.

"Hmmm." she mumbled then pulled the door open.

Chapter 5

We must learn who is gold and who is gold-plated!

Blu'Jai was impressed with the coffee shop's unique artistry. The place looked like a custom-created treasure with an accommodating staff that was treating people like family. They even had live music from local artists for the grand opening. Yella Beezy was even scheduled to make an appearance. The energy was on ten and Blu'Jai beamed with pride as her eyes searched for Natural. A few familiar faces gave her hugs and warm smiles, all of whom had flavorful mugs in their hands filled with unique coffee blends: caramel latte, cappuccino, macchiatos, and even blonde roast coffees that awaken the senses as gentle as the morning sun. When the band went into Daniel Caesar's *'Get You,'* Blu'Jai was really in her zone. She ordered a French Vanilla latte and rocked to the smooth sound of the brother on the mic. His sounds had folks' hips swinging and jumping the air like an invisible Michael B Jordan or Saweetie was in front of them.

Scanning the room, she spotted Natural and Kyron laughing and shooting the breeze with Tazzell and two other females that she didn't recognize. She grabbed her mug, put on her *Bitch, I'm in the building* smile, turned up her *my shit don't stank* walk, and headed in their direction.

What the hell is Tazz doing here anyway? she thought to herself. Blu'Jai knew that Tazz was cool with both Natural and Kyron, but Blu'Jai had just gotten off the phone with the bitch and she hadn't once mentioned that she was coming.

"Heeeyyy!!" Blu'Jai sang as she stepped into the circle making her presence known.

"Kyron, you've really outdone yourself with this place!" Blu'Jai complimented.

"Thank You!" Kyron gave a half smile. "Couldn't have done it without our brother here!" He grabbed Natural's shoulder and squeezed it. Both men were looking good as hell in their tailored Italian suits.

"Hey Natural! Hey Tazzell!" Blu'Jai spoke tossing Tazz a puzzling look, intending to give off *'what the fuck you doing here.'*

She had on a rose patterned sun dress that made her ass look like she had just gotten a Brazilian butt lift.

"Sup sis." Natural smirked.

"What's good Blu," Tazz said, picking up on the shade Blu'Jai was throwing her way, so she just threw that shit right back.

"When you're up in life, your friends get to know who you are. When you're down in life you get to know who your friends are." Tazzell said with a smile.

"Tazz, we just discussed that shit about me asking you to leave my house, if that's what all that riddle shit is about. So why you trying to murder the vibe on something dumb? That situation was like yesterday boo, so let's enjoy the moment!" Blu'Jai held her hand up as to signal stop.

"Oh, I'm cool, babe! Trust! But you just promise me that you'll stay cool up in here!" Tazz giggled. "I mean, this is a big day, and I'm excited for Kyron and Natural. This man has been through hell and back!" Tazz said. "Sat in a jail cell for three years, then after not even being out a whole month, he finds himself being co-owner of this fine establishment! I'd say that's pretty amazing, wouldn't you?"

"Co-owner?" Blu'Jai smiled. "I kind of figured something when I saw the sign out front with Natural's name on it!"

"Yeah and he managed to pull it off despite the fact that you stole all of his money!" Tazzell held up her hand to give Blu'Jai a high five.

"Fuck are you talking bout I stole his money?" Blu'Jai frowned, not believing her muthafuckan ears! "Rewind!" she spat with a look, daring Tazzell to repeat herself.

"Blu'Jai would you please excuse yourself." Kyron asked politely. "You are not welcome in our place of business."

"Fuck you mean I…ain't…welcome?!" Blu'Jai spat each word slowly.

"Look," Natural started in. "This is neither the place nor the time to have this conversation, so I'll be as brief as possible. I'm fully aware that you stole every penny of my money, and Kyron is fully aware of what used to be our relationship."

"Who told you about the money? Tazz?" Blu'Jai eyed her suspiciously.

"I damn sure did!" Tazz pipped in. "Natural's too good of a man to let a foul ass bitch like you win."

"So, you've been the snake the whole time?" Blu'Jai squinted at Tazz.

"Nah hun, I've been *real*! You've been the snake. Now Natural has a real woman on his team." Tazzell said.

"Let me guess? You?" Blu'Jai laughed.

"Correct! Ding, Ding, Ding!" Tazz laughed.

"Wow!" Blu'Jai eyed both Tazz and Natural. "All along, right under my nose huh?" Blu'Jai had a good mind to dash Tazzell with the hot Latte. "You know what," she sang. "I'm gooood. Like fa-real, fa-real! You two look cute together," Blu'Jai laughed. "I got the money; you can have the dick!" Blu'Jai popped turning on her heels to leave.

"Oh, and um Natural… I would advise you not to run up in it raw." She gave a warning brow. "She keeps a yeast infection. That's why her pussy always smell like dead fish and rotten eggs!

Invest in a gas mask boo!" Blu'Jai pulled out her Visa card. "Maybe I'll purchase one for you guys, after all I do have the money!!!"

Kyron shook his head and laughed to himself as Blu'Jai walked out the door.

Blu'Jai drove home in silence. She couldn't wait to get home so she could take her game face off. She had wanted to cry back at the coffee shop but had refused to let those fuckers see even one salty tear.

Tazz, I'm a get yo backstabbing ass, Blu'Jai said to herself.

After all they had been through, the bitch had done her dirty. That's probably how everyone knew Natural was coming home so fast. Those two snakes had been hissing with one another the whole while. Maybe Latoya Logan had been hinting around the shit the whole time. Every time Blu'Jai went up to Latoya's salon to get her hair done Latoya would make comments like if she were in Blu'Jai's shoes, she wouldn't feel comfortable with Tazz going to visit her dude alone and writing letters that she hadn't inspected with her own eyes. Blu'Jai passed it off as insecurity. Blu'Jai was secure with her shit, and Tazz was her girl. Blu'Jai hated that she didn't pay heed to the jewels Latoya had been dropping.

Instead of going home Blu'Jai decided to go to the Galleria mall. Shopping had always been therapeutic for her. *Fuck all them tricks!* she thought as she turned on a classic from Beyoncé: "Me, Myself, and I."

"Me, myself and I, that's all I've got in the end,
that's what I found out,
And it ain't no need to cry, I took a vow that from now on
I'm gone be my own best friend."

Blu'Jai sang as she pulled into the parking lot. She headed straight for the Gucci store. Several niggas' eyes burned holes in her, but none of them smelled like money, so she kept it pushing. Blu'Jai could smell money from a fuckin' block away.

"Damn girl! You are looking good!" she heard a deep voice compliment. Where you going?"

Blu'Jai turned to see who the sweet but nosy voice belonged to. She hated for niggas to be all up in her business. *Mind your own,* she thought, but smiled when she saw his face.

"Miles!" she cheesed. "What are you doing here?"

"Was about to go grab a couple new units. Where you on your way to?"

"The Gucci store." Blu'Jai said

"Cool, I'll roll. I look good in Gucci!" Miles popped.

"You damn sure do!" Blu'Jai agreed. "I know you don't do gossip but I gotta tell you about your girl."

"Who?" Miles frowned.

"The Tazz bitch!"

"Oh, okay. What's up?"

"Bitch put all my shit in the street with my man Natural, and now they like booed the fuck up! Shit is foul!"

"I know she grimy but damn." Miles said unfazed.

"Okkaaayyy!!" Blu'Jai sang. "But I've got the money, so I ain't even gone trip!" she flashed her Visa at Miles. "In fact, one of your outfits on me!' she winked.

"Okkaaayyy!! Miles mocked her tone with a laugh, and they headed for the Gucci store.

Blu'Jai tried on a few outfits and Miles gave her the thumbs up on each one. She would turn and made sure her ass looked good in each outfit, because she wouldn't dare buy anything that didn't compliment her most prized possession. After deciding on a few items, and Miles picking up a pair of shoes, belt and matching hat, they headed to the counter to get rung up. Blu'Jai passed the cashier her visa as she and Miles discussed the possibility of hanging out sometimes.

"Excuse me Ms. Ramos." the cashier interrupted. "I'm sorry to tell you but this card has been declined."

"That's got to be a mistake boo, I just used that card yesterday! Swipe it again." Blu'Jai smiled. The cashier did as she was asked yet the card declined again. "Well try this one and I'll call to straighten this out later." Blu'Jai passed her American Express Platinum Card. The cashier informed Blu'Jai that her American Express had declined too.

"I bet Natural has something to do with this!"

She turned to Miles with a frown. She quickly logged into her savings account on her phone and immediately went into a cold sweat. Her account read *zero*! Tears streamed down her face as she fought to breathe.

"Ma'am are you okay?" the cashier asked, but Blu'Jai had lost her voice.

Natural had got her with the only thing worse than the cross, the *doublecross*. Blu'Jai passed out right on the floor of the Gucci store.

Chapter 6

Those people who tried to bury you didn't know you were a seed.

Blu'Jai climbed out of her comfortable king-sized bed, not giving a fuck if she woke Miles up or not. He was in a blissful sleep on the left side of her bed. In fact, she hoped his ass would stir, because she was about tired of his shit. She took her index finger and dug her panties out of her ass with one quick swipe as she looked at the nigga she had been dealing with for the last three months. Blu'Jai sucked her teeth and shook her head in disgust.

Snatching her iPhone off her nightstand, she headed to the bathroom, closed the door behind her and sat on the toilet.

And to make matters worse, he always got to fall asleep on my side of the damn bed, she grumbled to herself as she waited for Natural to reply to the text that she had just sent him. It was a picture of her fresh and neatly trimmed pussy she had taken earlier that day.

Miles had taken up the slack of taking care of her, true enough, but he wasn't the only one. He was just the one she knew she could depend on to provide for her. She had no complaints as far as the money went, but the bedroom was another story. He was a one and done nigga. After ten minutes of action he was nutting, and after that one nut he was done. He would pull the same tired ass routine, same predictable ass moves. First, she was on her back while he ate her pussy, then he'd dish out about ten pumps in missionary. Next, it's "Blu'Jai turn over and let me get that ass from the back." Then it was four or five pumps and two ass claps on his dick before he was passing out into a deep sleep. Blu'Jai knew she had some good pussy; she'd been told so many times, but her good pussy was no excuse for premature ejaculation and poor performance. To be honest that's just some downright selfish shit to be dishing out half ass fucks. Then have the nerve to ask her who's pussy it was, while humping away at a hundred miles an hour.

Come on dude! Are you fucking serious? She'd crack to herself, If *I told you whose it was, you'd be ready to fight on me!* She'd giggle inside, "It's yours Daddy!" Blu'Jai would humor him, ready for his ten-minute ride to be over. She HATED one and done brothers.

    At 27, Blu'Jai's body was still tight. Her mocha skin was stretchmark-free and flawless. She stood five-foot, with a small waist and a thick apple bottom. Her hairstyles varied from short to long with the help of Latoya Logan's Diamonds in a Bundle hair. She could transform into any look. By most men's standards she was a dime, although some would disagree, since niggas done started coming out with all these songs about being independent, having good credit, and all that other lame ass shit. Blu'Jai's credit was so jacked, she couldn't even get a loan to buy a pack of chewing gum. Too many car repossessions and broken apartment leases on her credit report. Finding a job had been virtually impossible since she now had a criminal record. She had been working as a security guard in the Galleria when she got arrested for boosting clothes out of Nordstrom. She had no idea how she had gotten caught, because she had been stealing out of different stores since her first day on the job. The extra money she'd get for the merchandise she'd come home with really came in handy, because those checks wasn't shit. Until she could find another job, her job would be to keep lame ass Miles pussy whipped. She was just going to have to fake it until she made it. This was her mindset.

She received a text from Natural.

Natural's text said, *That's how you feel?*

Blu'Jai responded, *trying to get up with you later tonight.*

Natural: That's what's up! Just hit me when you good.

Blu'Jai smiled at the thought of the A-1 dick she had set up. Natural had a big dick that he knew how to work, could fuck as long as Blu'Jai needed him to, and ate her pussy like it was his favorite meal. Blu'Jai sat her phone on the sink, pulled the white tank she was wearing over her head, and slipped out her panties. She looked at the time on her phone before she climbed into the tub for a hot shower.

It's ten thirty, she thought to herself. *I got to find a way to get rid of this nigga, so I can get mines in.* She continued to think as the water cascaded down her firm breasts. The warm water was doing a number on her and she felt the tension she was feeling minutes ago begin to leave her body. She closed her eyes and rubbed the thick bodywash all over her smooth skin. She heard her bathroom door open, and the sound of piss filling the toilet broke her trance.

"Damn Blu, hurry that shit up! I need to jump in there really quick so I can go meet this nigga that just text me," Miles stated in a lazy voice before flushing the toilet.

"Okay, Daddy. I didn't know you had to leave." she said and started rinsing the soap off. The news was music to her motherfuckin' ears.

Miles was a D-Boy who hustled twenty-four seven. He wasn't a big timer, but he was a far stretch from a cornerboy fighting for scraps. Blu'Jai didn't have a problem with him hustling if he A: didn't bring his business into her apartment, and B: didn't have a problem with bringing her his bread.

"What's up with Natural?" Miles asked from the other side of the shower curtain.

"We still friends, why?" Blu'Jai asked.

"Cuz you got a text from the nigga on your phone! Dats why." Miles sounded like he was getting upset.

"Daddy, that ain't nothing, so stop tripping!" she calmly injected, trying to defuse anything before it could get started while turning off the water.

It was crazy how she and Tazzell had basically swapped niggas. Blu'Jai felt like she had gotten the short end of the stick, but shit was hard, and she needed a money flow.

"Well what the fuck this nigga want this time of night?" Miles asked in a menacing tone. "I swear you bitches can't be trusted as far as I can see you!" he laughed.

Suddenly the shower curtain came crashing down on top of her. She screamed as she slipped and fell in the wet tub. A wave of panic swept through her when she saw the blood swirling down the drain with the soapy water. Miles jumped on top of her and trapped her in the small tub. His body weight and the shower curtain had her covered like her grandmother's homemade quilt.

"The fuck?" Blu'Jai screamed terrified.

"Bitch!!! Why this nigga texting you, asking if you want him to pick you up some Ecstasy pills before he comes by?" Miles growled. "Huh?!" he bit down hard on his bottom lip and smashed her skull into the tub.

"Miles please! I told you, Natural just a friend!" Blu'Jai cried out in pain, barely able to breathe.

"Just friends huh?" Miles growled pressing her head even harder against the floor of the tub before climbing out and snatching up Blu'Jai's phone again. "After this nigga fucked over you! Left you broke! Got you put out yo fuckin' condo and had yo stupid ass homeless you gone still sit up here and tell me yall fuckin' friends?!" Miles screamed as she gasped for air, then finally left the bathroom.

She climbed out of the tub with tears falling from her eyes and walked into her bedroom to find Miles sitting on her bed going through her text messages.

"You still fuckin this nigga. Ain't cha hoe?!" Miles fumed. "Friends, huh bitch?" he spat, eyes darting back and forth from the screen to Blu'Jai.

That's how you feel…trying to get up with you later tonight.

"Yeah," he nodded his head. "That's how you feel? That's how you moving bitch? *I'm tryna get up with chu tonight?* Sho don't sound like a fuck date to me!" he spat as he read the messages out loud.

He grabbed his Polo jeans off the floor and snatched the leather belt out the loops. "Ima beat yo ass bitch! You supposed to be my bitch and you out here hoeing! Nah bitch! You outta line popping yo pussy while you shine off my dime! You and Tazzell just gone hoe the shit out huh? May tha best hoe win type shit!"

Blu'Jai took off running through her apartment butt naked trying to avoid the whipping Miles was so eager to hand out. This wasn't the first time he had gotten abusive with her, but it was the first time he had ever taken it to this extent. He was livid.

"Help! Please! Somebody help!" she screamed as she struggled to unlock the front door. She howled at the top of her lungs when she felt the sting of the leather across her back. "Please Miles! I'm sorry! I won't do it again! I promise!"

POP! She felt the sting again.

"Oh God!" she cried as she finally managed to get the door unlocked.

He grabbed one of her arms and tried to pull her away from the door, but she mustered up enough strength to turn the knob before he could do so, and the door swung wide open. Miles let her arm go and raced to the door to close it, but Blu'Jai managed to beat him to it and ran outside. Miles ran up behind her and pushed her down on the concrete. He began swinging the belt furiously and violently across her arms, back and ass cheeks.

"You want all these muthafuckas in our business, fine with me! It ain't gone stop this ass whipping bitch!" Miles fumed as he continued to swing his belt.

Blu'Jai was kicking and screaming like a two-year-old. She couldn't even remember her own mama giving her an ass whipping like the one she was receiving from a man that she didn't even love; and out of all nights, why ain't nobody outside! Blu'Jai thought to herself as the belt came crashing down on her again.

"Please, God! Save me!" she begged mercifully.

"God!" Miles spat. "God don't aid the muthafuckin' Devil, bitch!"

Cars were starting to pull up and people were finally starting to come out of their apartments. God had heard her prayers and the neighbors had heard her cries. A small crowd had started forming around the drama, and everyone was putting their two cents in.

"Beat that ass homeboy! I know whatever she did, she won't do it again!" Blu'Jai could hear one dude encourage.

"Hold them legs!" another guy advised.

Blu'Jai couldn't believe her ears. What the fuck had happened to days were people loved one another, helped each other, or even had a once of compassion in their hearts.

"Call the police!" Blu'Jai begged as Miles' fury continued to rain down on her.

"Police?! Bitch we don't snitch around here!" a female boasted. "This karma coming to yo ass for fucking my baby daddy! Didn't think I knew huh? Take that shit! Snitch bitch!" Blu'Jai still couldn't believe her ears.

Everyone was more concerned with getting video footage to post on Instagram Live than trying to help. One would have thought that she was a reality star with all the phones videoing her. She turned her head to avoid the strike that was coming towards her face with the belt Miles had in his hand when suddenly, a miracle happened! It looked to be a ray of light that appeared, and God had sent her the help that she pleaded for. She spotted a young teenage boy walking around the corner of the apartment complex. He had a backpack over his shoulder and looked to be eighteen or nineteen. Blu'Jai had seen the youngster around plenty of times, so she knew he lived nearby.

"Help! Please help meee!!!" she screamed in a strained voice as her eyes locked with his.

Her prayers were answered when she saw the young boy drop his bag and break out into a mad dash towards her direction. He ran with more speed and grace than she had ever seen, weaving through the crowd, when he suddenly took flight and tackled Miles so hard that he howled. The young boy was back on his feet quickly, but Miles being a student of the streets hood tactics, he quickly wrapped the belt around the teenager's foot and snatched him back down in one swift motion.

"Young ass nigga!" Miles hissed through clenched teeth. "You wanna get in my binnis, then you can get the binnis too!" he spat.

The young boy was outweighed by a good fifty pounds. Miles knew the kid couldn't match his strength, so he dropped his belt and began punching the boy in his face with his fist like the kid was a grown man. Blu'Jai got up off the ground and started running back towards her apartment. She thought to herself, *fuck them,* but as she ran about four or five steps, she abruptly turned around because her conscious wouldn't let her leave the boy. She quickly shot back and picked up the belt off the ground. Like a cat she eased up and hooked it around Miles' neck from behind. She applied as much pressure as she could, which was only enough for the youngster to escape the beat down he was receiving. The young boy kicked Miles in the nut sack and that sent him crumbling to the ground, allowing them both to run for cover and get the hell away from him.

"Come on, hurry!" Blu'Jai yelled.

The boy followed Blu'Jai as they sprinted up the stairs, back to her apartment and locked Miles outside. Seconds later Miles was kicking and beating on the door like a freaking wild man.

"Open this muthafucka up before I kick it down!" he threatened.

Blu'Jai ran to her bedroom and grabbed the .22 out of the bag in her closet where she kept her gun. Her hands trembled as she loaded bullets into the clip. Popping in the full magazine, she ran back to the front.

"Miles leave before I call the police and empty the clip in your ass!" Blu'Jai warned meaning every word.

"Give me my got damn clothes and my car keys bitch! I'm gone leave, just give me my shit!" Miles shouted.

"I'm not giving you anything! Are you fuckin' serious? Get yo ass away from my door, and I'm not going to tell you again!" Blu'Jai warned.

She was standing with her legs spread like police officers do with two hands on her piece. It was none of that sideways television gangsta shit! She was ready to fire at Miles through her apartment door if she heard any more signs of movement from him. Miles took heed to her warnings and he left. Blu'Jai took a deep breath, called the police and then lowered the gun down to her side with ease. The youngster was mesmerized by the gorgeous woman. Her physique gave him butterflies. Blu'Jai was certainly a grown woman, and it was his first time looking at a woman her age, in the nude. His dick sprung to life.

"You okay?" he asked, looking at the scratches and whelps all over her body while trying to hide the bulge in his pants.

"Yeah, I think I am. Thank you for helping me. I'm sorry that I got you caught up in my shit." She exhaled deeply.

"Oh, I'm straight. It probably looked worse than it felt." Then he started to massage the side of his face where Miles had hit him.

"Why don't you have a seat and let me put some clothes on." Blu'Jai suggested.

"Well I have school in the morning, so I probably need to be heading home." he said nervously.

"School? Boy, how old are you?" Blu'Jai asked as she walked into her bedroom and grabbed a pair of sweatpants to put on and a t-shirt from her dresser.

"I'm eighteen." he answered.

"What school do you go to?" she questioned, walking back into the living room fully dressed and plopping down on the couch.

She crossed her leg and patted the cushion next to her for him to come and sit down.

"You can sit for a second, damn. I almost got you killed, the least I can do is find out who you are."

"Well I go to Carter High School." he answered, taking a seat next to her. He was noticeably still amped.

"What grade?" she asked, slicking her hair into a ponytail with her hands.

"Senior, I graduate this year."

"Really?" she smiled. "That's quite an accomplishment. What's the plan after you graduate?"

"College! I've already committed to attending Texas Christian University." he answered proudly.

"TCU? You've already picked a school?" Blu'Jai nodded her approval.

"Yes ma'am." His voice was sounding more relaxed as he continued to chat with her.

"Committed? What you mean? As in already having a scholarship or something?" She asked with a raised brow.

"Yeah, I play football." he answered. "My father went to TCU, so I kinda wanted to follow in his footsteps.

"Football? Well that explains the impressive tackle you put on Miles."

Blu'Jai then asked the youngster to hang around out of fear that Miles would come back, but the more they continued to talk, the more interesting she found the young man. It didn't hurt that he was built like an NFL player.

Still talking to the young boy, thoughts of Miles were parading in her head. The money Miles dished out was decent, but it damn sure wasn't worth all the emotional breakdowns she had because of him, the beatings that she had endured, and all the other mishaps and issues that he had bombarded her with. He was worse than a fuckin' female with jealous tendencies. Blu'Jai shook her head. This was it. *I'm leaving his bitch ass alone for real this time!* Blu'Jai promised herself.

"So, what's your name and what position do you play?" Blu'Jai quizzed and she was a little more intrigued this time.

"My name is Tedrick, and I play quarterback."

"Oh okay. Any good?" She gave him a look that was a playful frown, twisting up one side of her face.

"I've been a McDonald's All-American for three years. I'm the number one quarterback in the nation." he boasted.

She quickly changed her facial expression to a one of genuine surprise

"Oh! Really?" Blu'Jai smiled. "Maybe I'll get a chance to see you play one day. When is your next game?"

"It's Friday."

"You can go on YouTube and type in Tedrick Moss to watch a five-minute video of my highlights."

"That's great! I'll look on there and see how you are getting it in, with your cute self. I bet you got a thousand of those young girls at school all on you." she teased him.

He just smiled and chuckled. Blu'Jai noticed how beautiful his smile was.

"Yeah, I figured that!" she said playfully, punching his arm. "Are you ok?" she looked him over to see if there were any physical bruises.

"Yes ma'am, I'm fine." he replied, glancing at his watch, then standing up.

"Oh boy, stop that 'yes ma'am' stuff. I'm not that old! Call me Blu'Jai. You're so respectful though, I like that." Blu'Jai said. These new kids seemed to have lost all sense of respect, so it was refreshing to see that Tedrick had what most was lacking.

"Well I better get going. It's been a long day to say the least." he chuckled.

"How do you get to school in the mornings?"

"I ride the athletic bus, because I have to be there early to hit the weight room and work out."

"What time?" she asked. She started thinking back to her high school days. She was a hot mess back then. Thick and fine, and you couldn't tell her shit.

"The bus comes at five-thirty, so I can be there by six."

Blu'Jai glanced at the clock on the wall. "Where do you stay?" as she was doing a lot of calculating in her head.

"I live with my mom right around the corner from you." Tedrick waved his thumb in the direction in which he lived.

"Let me see your phone." Blu'Jai ordered.

He pulled it out of his pocket and handed it to her. She dialed her number and locked it into his phone.

"This is my number. Call me when you get up in the morning and I will take you to school so you don't have to ride the bus."

"You don't have to do that," Tedrick assured.

"I want too! So, call me, okay," Blu'Jai insisted.

Walking Tedrick to the door she said, "Call me when you get home to let me know you got in safe."

"Okay." he said glancing down at the name she'd locked in his phone. "Blu'Jai Ramos?" he said loud with a cheesy smile.

"Yep that's me!" she beamed. "And thanks again for everything."

Tedrick threw up the deuces and headed home. Blu'Jai locked the door and smiled.

'Damn that's a young fine ass nigga; and he aint out here tryna be a gangsta like most of these other young guys,' she thought to herself as she went into the bedroom and grabbed her iPad to get on YouTube.

Blu'Jai couldn't believe her eyes as she watched his highlights. This boy looks like Patrick Mahomes, the way he's running around. She thought Tedrick was a phenomenal player, and obviously he was; every college in the nation was trying to recruit him. He was a five-star recruit, and by far the best high school quarter back Blu'Jai had ever seen. She was amazed at how easy he escaped tackles, how he seemed to outrun everyone on the field, and how he would make a sixty-yard pass look effortless. To say she was impressed would be an understatement. She watched the highlight video four or five times, and each time she found herself shaking her head about his great athletic ability. She heard her phone ring, so she jumped up and ran into the bedroom to find it.

"Hello." she answered, half-panting.

"Blu'Jai?" Tedrick's voice was on the other end of the phone, deep and sexy.

"Yes. So, you made it safe?"

"Yeah. I'm good."

Damn he sounds good' she thought to herself. "Great!" She smiled while checking some unread messages in her phone. "Hey, I just watched your highlights on You Tube" she said.

"So, what you think?" he was anxious to hear her response.

"I think if you work hard, you will make it as far as your heart desires."

He blushed and said thank you.

"Now get off this phone and go to bed." she ordered, sounding like a mother. "Don't forget to wake me up."

By this time, she was cheesing so hard her cheeks were hurting and she couldn't understand why, but the thing that she did notice was that he is a very handsome and talented young man.

Chapter 7

It's very rare to find someone who isn't full of shit.

Blu'Jai hung the shower rod and curtain back up, straightened the bathroom and called Natural. A good fuck is just what she needed to unwind after all the drama that had taken place the night before. She already paid the price, so she figured she may as well reap the reward. She was determined to get hers tonight, welted up body and all.

Despite their ups and downs, Natural was still the nigga. Blu'Jai loved his style and his rough yet smooth way of handling her. Thirty minutes after she called Natural, she found herself leaning over the back of her love seat with her ass towards him getting banged from behind. The mellow sound of Jacquees' music played through her stereo speakers while the sound of Natural's nut sack slapping her ass, and a slurping sound was coming from the stroke of his dick in her pussy. With each stroke, the thrust of them making love was more intoxicating than any drug could ever be. Sex with Natural was a great healing for Blu'Jai.

Natural bent his knees to get better leverage and grabbed Blu'Jai's thick hips as he put his pound game down to the fullest. His dick wasn't all that long, but it was thick and he knew exactly what to do with it.

"Damn Nat." she moaned. "You getting' all the way up in this pussy!" Blu'Jai whined in her baby voice as she stood on her tip toes to give Natural better access.

Fuck Tazz, she thought. *This dick has Blu'Jai's name all over it and it always will.*

Natural picked up the pace and started taking shorter, harder, and faster strokes.

"Shit baby, right there!"

She kept saying over and over, "Get this pussy Nat." Then she screamed as she rocked her hips to meet his thrust.

"Take this dick, bitch!" Natural ordered as he grabbed one of her legs and propped it up on the back of the love seat. He slammed his dick in her pussy with a forceful pound that made her titties bounce wildly.

"Ooooh shit, Nat! Get this pussy, boy!" she cried.

He pulled out as far as he could without his dick fully exiting her, repositioned his dick, adjusted it in her pussy, and pounded her ass again.

"Uuuummm... Oh! God!" she moaned, as he paused for a couple seconds before banging her again.

He loved to watch the waves ripple through her fat asscheeks so much that he felt himself about to cum, and he did just that.

"Put this muthafucka in yo mouth." Natural said.

Slipping his dick out of her pussy, Blu'Jai quickly turned around, pulled the condom off his dick, then licked the shaft from his nut sack to the split on the big mushroom head. In one swift motion she had his whole dick in her mouth and Natural gasped in pure bliss because it felt so good as she found her rhythm. Blu'Jai knew she had some of the best head in Texas, and she prided herself for always giving a top notch performance. There is an art to sucking dick and she had it mastered. Most bitches gave head soft and slow, mimicking the way they liked to get their pussy ate. But she had learned over the years that men preferred it to be done hard and fast. It took a lot of practice and the use and development of her neck muscles to be able to do it just right, but she had acquired a head game that was fast and furious. Her head bobbed up and down on his dick like a well-oiled well machine.

"Agh shit ma!" Natural moaned as he grabbed the back of her head. "Damn bitch, Ima bout to nut!" he warned her as she continued to suck on his dick.

"Mmmhmmm… You sure are." she said with her baby voice, not missing a beat.

Natural exploded, released his cum in her mouth, and used the excess cum that she didn't catch inside her mouth for a lube to stroke his dick until it got even harder than the first time. It was a trick that she knew how to administer from her bag of goodies, and a good excuse for her not to swallow. Blu'Jai laid on her back for a second round of love making. Sex to be exact. Natural pushed her knees up to her chest and they went at it for another full hour. After the steamy second round, Blu'Jai went in the bathroom, flushing the used condoms and packages. *Never leave evidence behind*, she thought to herself.

"I enjoyed myself Natural, but I need to get some rest. So, call me when you get home to let me know you made it safe." She received personal enjoyment from fucking Natural's brains out just to spite Tazzell's thot ass.

"Oh, you got the dick now you kicking me out, huh?" he laughed.

"Ahh, it's like that? It's cool though." Natural teased. He knew she was still in her feelings, so he let it go.

"Now you know it aint even like that. It's just that I have to be up early in the morning." she yawned.

She had to admit she really did miss his ass, but he had done her dirty so there was no coming back from that. All he was good for now was his money and some good dick.

"Alright Blu." he said, kissing her on her forehead. "I'll call you."

SELFISH

$ $ $ $ $

It felt like her head had just hit the pillow when she heard her phone ring.

"Hello" she said in a groggy voice.

"It's Tedrick. I was just calling like you asked, but you can go back to sleep. I don't mind catching the bus." He had considered just sending her a text and now he wished he had because he felt bad about waking her up.

She sat up in her bed, "Boy stop playing." Blu'Jai grinned. Tedrick's voice was a welcomed sound in her ear, no matter what time of morning it was. She eased her hand down between her legs and rubbed her kitty.

"Come over after you get dressed and I will take you to school."

She hung up the phone and pulled herself out of bed. She jumped in the shower and threw on her pants and a wife beater Her hair was wrapped in a scarf, and she slipped her feet into her fuzzy pink sandals. Blu'Jai grabbed two eggs out the refrigerator and a half pack of turkey bacon. She scrambled the eggs and fried the bacon before making freshly buttered Texas toast. Tedrick knocked on the door, and when she opened it she led him into the kitchen to eat the breakfast she prepared. She poured herself a hot cup of coffee and a glass of orange juice for Tedrick. He sat his backpack in the empty chair at the table and took a seat.

"You didn't have to fix breakfast," he said as she sat the plate of eggs, bacon and toast and jelly in front of him.

"Boy, just eat," she told him, crossing her leg under her bottom before sitting in the chair across from him.

She gave him a playful annoyed look and watched him eat while she sipped her coffee. She thought it was cute how he demolished his food. *Just a young, growing boy*, she thought to herself as she grabbed his empty plate and told him to get his books. She knew she was old enough to be his mother, but she found Tedrick very attractive. His six-foot-three frame, the peach fuzz on his chin, as well as the stud earrings that he wore in both ears. He was dark chocolate and looked like he weighed about a hundred and fifty pounds. His clothes didn't really look expensive, but he dressed well enough to put his shit together nicely.

She grabbed her car keys and they both climbed into her Nissan Altima. She noticed Miles' cream-colored Jaguar still parked next to her car and made a mental note in her head to call his ass later. She couldn't wait to drop Tedrick off at school because she needed to make a phone call to Miles or send him a text telling him to come get his shit, his clothes and his car that was occupying a much-needed visitor parking space in her apartment complex.

Blu'Jai pulled up in front of the high school and started thinking about her own high school years. Those were some of the best years of her life.

"Have a good day; and you can hit me if you want to. I won't be doing anything." she said as Tedrick climbed out of the car.

She pulled off and texted Miles on her way home. The more she thought about Miles sorry ass the more she missed Natural.

You need to come get your shit nigga! and about a minute later she got a reply.

Miles in jail. Who dis?

She didn't reply. She just called down to the county jail when she got home and asked what they had Miles Jackson charged with.

"Assault on a police officer," the operator informed her.

Damn! I wonder what his stupid ass has done now. She thought about it but didn't really give a fuck, so the thought of it left her mind as quickly as it had entered.

Blu cleaned up her place then went to the hair salon and got her hair done before she stopped at the nail shop to get her mani and pedi. That took up most of her afternoon, but she decided to call Natural to see if he was up for a midday quickie, and of course he was down. Blu felt that there wasn't a nigga alive that can turn down her good pussy. The thought caused her to smile to herself.

After another great performance on both their parts, Blu'Jai flushed the condoms and jumped in the shower. They had only had sex for an hour this time around, but Natural's hour was far better than most niggas all-nighters. Natural didn't hang around long, so Blu'Jai found something else to occupy her time. She'd tried to text and call Kyron a million and one times, but he'd only replied to one text. In one text he said two words: *NOT INTERESTED*.

Motherfuck Kyron and that bitch ass coffee.

Blu'Jai was thinking to herself, *now what can I do since Natural has left?* She found herself sitting in the middle of her bed again, legs folded under her bottom, with her laptop in front of her. She watched Tedrick's highlight videos a few more times before deciding to leave and go watch him practice. She pulled up at the school in a pair of denim shorts, a plain, fitted white T-shirt, and a pair of leather wedge sandals. She stepped out of the car with Gucci shades on and a bottle of water, then she sashayed across the football practice field until she made it to a set of empty benches. She took a seat and crossed her legs as she scanned the field full of high school athletes.

"Damn!" she overheard one of the young boys say.

"Whose mama is that?" he asked his buddy standing next to him.

"Fuck if I know, but she fine as hell!" he said, dapping up his friend.

Blu'Jai just laughed to herself and shook her head. It was flattering that she can still turn the heads of such young guys at twenty-seven. After taking a quick selfie out on the field and posting it on Instagram, she wiped the sweat from her brow with her index finger as a coach approached her with the whistle around his neck and a clipboard under his arm. He looked to be around Blu'Jai's age. He was physically fit with his pecs showing through his sweaty t-shirt. He was also wearing a pair of shorts and a Carter Cowboy ball cap on his head.

"How are you today? May I help you? I'm Coach Griffen." he said, extending his hand to greet her. Blu'Jai shook his hand but didn't bother to stand up!

"Hi, I'm Blu'Jai and I hope it's not a problem with me watching you guys practice today."

He said, "no problem at all," smiling. "I figured that you were a reporter or something as pretty as you are. We get reporters out here daily and it can get to be a mad house once practice starts, so I just wanted to speak with you while time permits."

"Well Coach Griffen, I'm not a reporter, I just came to watch my neighbor Tedrick Moss."

Raising his eyebrows and bucking his eyes, Coach Griffen asked, "oh, really? He is a guy to watch, I'm proud of him. Everyone that comes out here is someway tied to him, either by interviewing him or trying to convince and persuade him to attend their college."

"I definitely think that he is a good athlete, but I haven't had the chance to see him play in person."

"Well Blu'Jai – and I hope that you don't mind that I call you by your first name - Homecoming is this weekend! That's going to be a good game against Dallas Skyline. I think you'd be missing a treat if you didn't come. Tedrick and his girlfriend Ayanna are going to be crowned Homecoming King and Queen."

Blu'Jai sighed. "His girlfriend?" she questioned trying not to sound so upset. She wanted to slap the shit out of Coach Griffen for even speaking such a blasphemous word. *GIRLFRIEND*! The word *GIRLFRIEND* felt like a ton of bricks on her tongue.

"Yeah, she's a cutie pie. She is a cheerleader and they've been hanging out since he first came here, which is a good thing to me because she helps me keep him grounded. It's easy to let the success that he's having go to your head."

"I'm sure." Blu'Jai's voice dripped attitude as she sucked her teeth. She tapped her foot repeatedly, closed her eyes and took a deep breath.

Coach shifted, yet stood firm before making his next statement. "I hope it isn't inappropriate if I asked you would you go out with me sometimes?"

"Of course not," she smiled. *I've actually been craving a giant lobster and a giant piece of cheesecake. Oh my God!*

Blu gave the coach her phone so he could store his numer. "I'll text you my number. You can call me anytime."

"Sounds good," the coach said eagerly, carefully punching each number into her phone, then locking Blu'Jai's number as soon as it appeared on his screen.

"I better get to practice, but I'll definitely get with you later," he said, shaking her hand.

"I'll be looking forward to it." She batted her eyes.

"It was nice meeting you." he blushed. Blu'Jai was by far one of the sexiest women he'd met in a good while.

"Likewise. Can you tell Tedrick that I'm here?" She gave him a knowing smile.

"You got it." he said before turning around jogging off like he just scored a Super Bowl touchdown. By the way coach was acting it wouldn't have surprised her one bit if he busted a funky end zone dance.

Blu'Jai watched the practice and was even more impressed by how gracefully Tedrick moved on the field. After practice, Tedrick walked over to Blu'Jai, but before he could make it over to her, Ayanna ran up behind him and slipped her arm around his waist. They both headed in Blu'Jai's direction.

"Hey, Blu'Jai, this is my girlfriend, Ayanna. Ayanna this is my neighbor I was telling you about, Blu'Jai."

Ayanna said energetically, "nice to meet you ma'am."

There was that word *GIRLFRIEND* again. Blu'Jai shook her head as she looked Ayanna up and down after shaking the thought of big facing the girl.

Blu'Jai smiled and said, "nice to meet you too. Tedrick I was expecting your call." She gave him a warning brow, but her fake smile was still in tact.

"Oh, I forgot. I just have been working so hard to get ready for this game on Friday." he admitted.

Blu'Jai was ready to go off. She was the temper tantrum Queen when she didn't get her way. She wanted to snatch his ass up and let it be known who was running shit, but she held her emotions in check.

"Well come on, I came to pick you up." she said as she shifted her weight to one leg.

"Oh, I'm going to have to pass. Yanna and I usually ride the bus home together," he replied, dropping his arm over her shoulders.

Blu'Jai squinted her eyes in Ayanna's direction and sucked her teeth. "Well I can take her home too." Blu'Jai offered reluctantly.

What she wanted to do was snatch that arm right off of that little bitch's shoulder. Blu'Jai was from the hood, and when you're from Oak Cliff, it wasn't shit to hand a bitch a can of *I'LL CLOWN YO ASS!* She wanted to get him away from this young hooker anyway. She had no idea why she was jealous, but she was. Like Coach Griffen said, she was a cutie, but in Blu'Jai's eyes, Ayanna was only a little girl. Coach Griffen walked by and winked while slapping Tedrick on the ass.

"Good practice kid," he said. "Gotta continue to work on getting the ball out of your hands a little quicker though."

Tedrick nodded and made a mental note to work harder on that part of his game.

"The ride sounds good to me. I don't really feel like riding the bus today anyway." Ayanna said, playfully slapping Tedrick on the ass like the coach had just done.

Tedrick climbed in the backseat, letting Ayanna sit up front with Blu'Jai. Ayanna gave Blu instructions to her house, and when they arrived Tedrick got out the car to walk her to the door like a perfect gentleman would. Blu'Jai smirked to herself and smacked her lips when she saw Tedrick kiss Ayanna goodbye. He jumped into the front seat and thanked her for dropping Ayanna off.

They rode back to Blu'Jai's apartment in silence. When they arrived, Tedrick grabbed his book bag and closed the car door. She unlocked the door and disarmed the alarm to her apartment.

"Go ahead and knock out your homework, and I'll fix your dinner." she said, dropping her purse on the kitchen table and heading towards the freezer to pull out some boneless chicken breasts.

"I really need to go home and let my mom know that I'm straight and take a shower." he said.

"Call your mom and tell her that you're over here around the corner. You can take a shower over here! I have some sweats you can put on."

Tedrick called his mom then jumped in the shower. She laid out a pair sweats and a big towel for him on her bed. When he got finished, he came out the bathroom.

"Where do you put the dirty towels?" he asked.

"Did you clean up that tub?" She teased him with a warning look.

"Not yet," he confessed. He was embarrassed that he hadn't.

"Make it happen Mr., then homework! Dinner will be ready by the time you get finished. You need to put on a pound or two anyway before you get hurt out there playing football," Blu'Jai said to him, eying his small chest and narrow waist.

"Weight will slow me down." he told her before slipping back into the bathroom to clean the tub.

Blu'Jai set the table and they both ate the chicken breast, mashed potatoes and mixed vegetables she had prepared. She had managed to learn to be a pretty decent cook.

"So, do you have any siblings?" she asked as she put a spoonful of potatoes in her mouth.

"No, I'm an only child." Tedrick was actually enjoying Blu'Jai's company. She was a grown woman. Her vibe and conversation were a lot different from the chicks his age.

"Me too." she said not knowing the effect she was having on him.

"Can I ask you something? Tedrick probed.

"Only if I can ask you something." she cheesed.

"Okay. How old are you?"

"I'm twenty-seven." Blu'Jai laughed. "Old lady, huh?" She joked and stood up. She did a slow turn to show off her thick curvy ass and clapped her ass cheeks together twice softly as to say 'I know' in booty talk then she sat back down.

"You don't look your age at all." His dick sprung to life. Her ass looked so soft, so juicy. But he kept his comments to himself.

"You're so quiet now, but on the field you're like a whole different person. You seem to be in total control of everything out there!"

"I have to be. The quarterback is the leader of the team and I have to play with confidence if I want the guys to follow me." Tedrick said defensively.

"I can understand that." Blu'Jai nodded. She gave him a cold look. A stare that was filled with the promise that she was serious as fuck. "I'm a control freak myself, to be honest. I love to be the boss. So, what's up with this little girlfriend of yours? Are you two very close?" She poked at the air with their fork in his direction.

"Yeah, that's my boo. We've been together since the 6th grade. She's cool, and for the most part I can trust her. My momma likes her, and I've always heard that moms spot the good ones and the bad ones. I know that once I go pro it would nearly be impossible to find a woman who doesn't have a secret agenda."

"Sooo, that's your dream, going to NFL?" She asked.

"Yeah. But I know a lot of guys don't make it, and you need to have a plan after, so I'm going to take advantage of the free college education."

"What kind of grades do you make?" she asked, astonished by his maturity.

"I've been an honor student all my life." He stated proudly. Tedrick knew that despite how good he was on the field, his education was just as important. If he made it big, he'd have to be smart enough to manage his money. If he didn't make it to the NFL, he had to be educated enough to make a living doing something else.

"I'm impressed. Now back to Ladonna." Blu'Jai blurted out, making a circle in the air with her fork.

"You mean Ayanna?" he corrected.

"Yeah whatever the little girl name is." Blu'Jai said waving her fork.

"Are you two having sex? If I'm not being too personal." she squinted, her eyes and awaited a response.

"No, she's still a virgin. I don't want to push her into anything she doesn't want to do." His eyes averted hers.

"So, you're telling me that you guys have been together since the 6th grade and haven't had sex not once?" Blu'Jai smiled.

"No. She's trying to concentrate on school right now. She does pretty good and wants to get a degree, so we agreed to wait."

"Until when?" Blu'Jai continued firing question after question.

"Until we get married."

"Married? So, you're a virgin too?"

He smiled and shook his head no.

"I should have known that answer." She laughed. "Cheater!"

"Only once, only once!" he said in defense of himself, holding up the palm of his hand as a sign of truth.

"Okay Mr. Man!" She said standing to the clear the table.

"I won't keep you up any longer. Call me and wake me up in the morning so I can take you to school."

"Okay, and thanks for everything," he said, grabbing his book bag.

"Bae stop all that!" she teased. "Come give me a hug before you go."

He wrapped his long arm around her and patted her back. His body hadn't fully matured, but he felt good in her arms. She was holding her ticket to life in the lap of luxury.

Chapter 8

You get what you focus on, so focus on what you want.

After a spectacular performance at the homecoming game, Tedrick was in every newspaper and on every news channel. He was even on the cover of Sports magazine, dubbing him the greatest high school quarterback Texas had ever seen. And he still had another year to showcase his talent before college. He was even scheduled to do an interview with ESPN's TV personality Stephen A. Smith.

Blu'Jai continued to fix his breakfast every morning, take him to school, and pick him up. It was a surprise that Ayanna became jealous of their relationship, and it was becoming a problem for Tedrick.

"You don't need to stress that relationship. You have dreams and goals to pursue." Blu'Jai would often tell him.

Blu'Jai started boosting clothes and sneakers for Tedrick, so his wardrobe would be official. He even had a closet full of new clothes at her house since they were spending more and more time together. She still gave Natural the pussy on a regular basis while Tedrick was at school, just to spite Tazzell, and she had even added coach Griffen to her list of fuck buddies when she could squeeze him in. She had a high sex drive that she prioritized, like her dream of living the champagne life.

Blu'Jai looked in the mirror and loved the reflection that looked back at her. It was Halloween and Tedrick invited her to a Halloween party that one of his friends was throwing. She wasn't too excited about going to hang out with a bunch of high school kids, but this was the first time he'd asked her to go somewhere with him, so it was like a first date for her, and she wasn't about to turn that down. Her costume was simple, yet sexy as hell. Tonight, she was Kat woman. She had on an all-black catsuit that hugged every curve of her body. She had on black thigh-high, high-heeled leather boots, black leather gloves that came up to her elbows, and a long ponytail that hung past her plump ass. She drew cat whiskers on her face and slipped on the black Catwoman's mask before going to answer her door to let Tedrick in. He was dressed as Superman, and Blu'Jai noticed that his body had thickened up in the month she had been cooking for him. He looked good and filled out the blue spandex suit he was wearing as well. He had on red boots, the "S" on his chest, the red cape…I mean, the whole hook up. She had hit Kyron up to see if they could hang out afterwards, but again, he wouldn't reply.

"You look nice," she said, hugging him. His hard body felt good against hers, and he was smelling good just like she liked.

"You do too, are you ready?" he asked, fighting the temptation to squeeze her ass.

"Yeah. let me lock up." She said locking the door.

She caught Tedrick staring at her ass and grinned. She backed her thick cheeks into Tedrick's crotch like it was an accident so he could feel what heaven was like. And she too was impressed with how his dick felt up against her.

"Here, you drive since you know where the party is." she said, handing him the keys.

"Me?! I don't even have a license!" he explained.

"Can you drive?" she asked, tossing him a quizzical look.

"Yeah - but I don't want to get you in trouble. And I'm tryna keep my name and character on point because they dig, dig, dig to find a flaw in anything an athlete does."

"Boy! Just don't be speeding!" she warned.

He opened the passenger door and let her in, then jumped behind the wheel.

"This party is going to be as hot as you look!" he grinned excitedly.

The vibe was perfect. Tedrick felt like the muthafuckin' man as he sunk into the soft leather seats.

"So, you think I look hot?" she asked seductively, reaching over and rubbing between his thighs, making circles in the area inches away from his dick.

"Hell yea!" he said, as he pulled out of the apartment complex with his Lil Man standing at attention.

Blu'Jai patted his thigh twice when she saw the print and removed her hand. She just relished in the mere fact that she was in control.

They arrived at the party, and everybody was showing love to Tedrick for his costume and his mysterious date.

"That ain't Ayanna is it? It can't be!" one of his friends asked Tedrick in what he thought was a whisper as he stared at Blu'Jai's ass.

"Nah dawg, this a friend of mine. Ayanna been tripping lately." Tedrick beamed at the amount of attention Blu'Jai was receiving. This was a real-life grown ass woman.

"Man, Catwoman fine as hell. You mind if I take a picture with her?" one of his teammates asked, hoping for a chance to get closer to the dime piece.

"Ask her, bro. I'm sure she won't mind." Tedrick said with a smile. "She cool, real down to earth." he added.

His friend asked Blu'Jai to pose for the camera, so she grabbed Tedrick and got down on her hands and knees. Arched her ass in the air like Eartha Kitt while Tedrick did his Superman pose behind her with his chest out and fist balled up on his hips.

"That's a hot pose!" his friend screamed over the loud music. "I'm 'bout to add these to my Instagram page!" he said with a smile.

Blu'Jai was showing out. Although she was almost 30, she was still flexible as hell and decided to put her skills on display. She got up, put her ass to the camera and kicked her leg up on Tedrick like she was trying to climb up his body as she looked over her shoulder and smiled. His friend snapped that shot as well, then suddenly Ayanna tapped Tedrick on the shoulder.

"Can I speak with you please?" she said with her arms folded across her chest, as she shot a mean look at Blu'Jai. Blu'Jai caught the look and threw that shit right back.

"Sure. Can you excuse me for a second Blu'Jai?" he asked.

"No problem. Take your time honey!" she said first flirtatiously, just to agitate the young girl. "Lil bitch got me fucked up." Blu'Jai mumbled.

"Come over to the computer and I will print you a copy of these, Catwoman." Tedrick's friend said as he led the way to the printer with his digital camera.

"What's this shit you're trying to pull Tedrick?" Ayanna screamed with tears in her eyes.

"Why you tripping? I don't even know what you're talking about."

Ayanna was dressed like Nicki Minaj with a loud pink wig and a skin-tight space age outfit. She was holding her own in the looks department as well, and had her share of guys chasing her too.

"I'm talking about you and this old ass lady you always up under!" Blu'Jai saw Ayanna screaming and pointing in her direction.

"It ain't like that Ayanna. And you know we been through too much to be at each other like this."

"That's what I thought too, but I don't like or trust her. You shouldn't either. What is an old bitch like that doing at this party, anyway?"

"Because I invited her." Tedrick said defensively.

"Tedrick, the woman is damn near thirty! Hanging out with high school kids! Think man! That's one of the reasons I always loved you, because you can think. So why are you unable to see she is no good?! I bet she's trying to use you for a free ride, and suddenly you want to act dumb. Tedrick, now ain't the time to be getting stupid! Leave that bitch alone!" Ayanna jabbed her finger in the air in Blu'Jai's direction.

"Is there a problem over here?" Blu'Jai stepped up having heard enough of the temper tantrum Ayanna was having. "I heard my name, so I decided to come over." She shifted her weight to one leg. She looked Ayanna up and down to let her know she really don't want these problems.

"Nobody said your name lady." Ayanna rolled her neck and hissed. "I was talking to my boyfriend, ma'am!"

"So, I wasn't the bitch you were referring to?" Blu'Jai asked coolly. "And ain't shit old about me except the type of ass whippings I pass out."

"As a matter fact you were!" Ayanna stated, getting sick of Blu'Jai. "You the bitch I'm talking about, and I don't have a problem with knocking dust from yo old ass, so don't test me!" she warned.

"Sweetheart you haven't seen a bitch yet, but just hang around honey." Blu'Jai said, dismissing the young girl. "Bye Felicia!"

Blu'Jai smiled a devilish grin then focused her attention back on Tedrick.

"Tedrick look! These pics came out nice. I'm going to post them on my page," she beamed, handing him the pictures they'd just taken.

Ayanna turned around and stormed off. "Don't even worry about calling me no more nigga!" she screamed. Tedrick had crushed her heart, and the shit hurt.

"Yanna!!! he screamed after her.

"Let's go Tedrick! This supposed to be a party, not a soap opera." Blu'Jai fanned Ayanna away like a pesky fly.

Blu started to dance really sexy in front of him, so he decided to just call Ayanna after the party. They danced a few songs before Blu'Jai went to the restroom. When she came back, Tedrick was with a group of young guys drinking beers. Blu'Jai marched right over to him and snatched the beer out of his hand. Beer flew out the bottle, dousing Tedrick and his friends, but Blu'Jai didn't give a lovely fuck. She felt like she needed to wear several hats when it came to Tedrick, and right now she was in mommy mode.

"What the hell are you doing?" she asked with the scowl on her face.

"I was just drinking a beer because I have a lot on my mind." Tedrick frowned, somewhat embarrassed by how Blu'Jai was carrying on.

"You don't need to be drinking. I don't care what these other knuckleheads do, but you ain't about to start no shit like that!" she scolded, tossing the bottle in the trash. "I will kick your ass all over this party. Do you hear me?"

Tedrick nodded shamefully. She was all up in his grill before she tossed his friends a defensive look.

"I'm ready to go!" Blu'Jai said, folding her arms across her chest.

Tedrick blew out a deep sigh, said his goodbyes, and left with Blu'Jai. He wanted to tell Blu'Jai to go fuck herself, but the warning look she gave him dared his ass to even keep entertaining the thought.

Ayanna sobbed uncontrollably when she saw Tedrick climb in the driver seat of Blu'Jai's car. He didn't notice her, but Blu'Jai did, so she reached over and pulled Tedrick's seatbelt across his lap then fastened him in. She then winked at the weeping young girl as they drove away.

Tedrick checked the text he received while driving once they made it to the apartment:

Superman my ass! You've got the right costume on though; CAPTAIN SAVE A HOE! Ayanna texted. He shook his head and sighed a deep breath.

"Who was that?" Blu'Jai asked, already knowing the answer to the question.

"Ayanna." Tedrick sucked his teeth.

"What did she say?" Blue Jai questioned.

"Nothing." he said.

Tedrick didn't even want to talk about it. He knew Ayanna was hurt, and he felt her pain. They had been together so long that they were connected like that.

"When I ask you something you answer that shit!" Blu'Jai practically jumped over into his face. "I'm tired of playing with you, Tedrick! Now what did the bitch say?"

"She said that my costume wasn't Superman, it was Captain Save a Hoe." he answered in a near whisper.

Blu snatched his phoned and texted Ayanna herself:

This is Blu! Stop texting this phone, cuz I'm about to block yo ass! She blocked Ayanna's number and tossed the phone back to Tedrick.

"Don't even respond to that childish shit. You need to stop playing with little girls and get you a real woman anyway! You're a real dude, and you're not on the same level as your friends. You're a man, and you need a woman that is capable of holding you down." she calmed back into her comfort zone.

"I'm starting to think that myself." Tedrick said. Ayanna was cool but she was still coming into her own, while Blu'Jai had already arrived.

They made it back to Blu'Jai's apartment and she locked the door behind them.

"Come here and let me show you how a grown woman, a real woman is supposed to treat you."

She squinted her eyes and licked her lips. She could already taste his young ass. She was about to eat his fine ass alive! Blu'Jai grabbed his hand and lead him into her bedroom. She was about to turn his young ass out, take him places he had never been, and show him things that he had never seen.

"Since it's Halloween, we may as well keep the party going." she said as she went into a dresser drawer that was filled with tricks. "Excuse me a second, let me run to the bathroom really quick." she added.

Tedrick sat on the edge of the bed thinking about Yanna until Blu'Jai stepped back into the room wearing only a red thong, the black thigh boots, and a matching lace bra and whip.

"What are you going to do with that whip?" Tedrick asked laughing.

She looked sexy as hell, but she had lost her mind if she thought she was going to use that on him.

"Whip your ass if you don't obey your mistress!" she said frankly, before cracking the whip close to his leg. She paced back and forth like a lion stalking her prey, her eyes trained on Tedrick. "Now take that shit off so I can look at that body!" she ordered.

Her face was serious and assertive. Tedrick did as he was told and stripped down to his boxers. Blu'Jai shook her head disapprovingly.

"I said all of it!" she screamed, cracking the whip again.

When he dropped his boxers Blu'Jai almost fainted. This young boy had a dick that seemed to stretch for miles. He had a grown man dick, and her mouth watered at just the sight of it. Now, she knew it was best that she took Tedrick off Ayanna's hands, because he was entirely too much for her. Hell, Blu'Jai was afraid that he would give her problems herself, with that Louisville slugger he was working with; but experience had taught her that having a gigantic dick wasn't all in all.

"You only speak when I tell you to. You do exactly what I tell you to, and you refer to me as ma'am or boss lady tonight! That's how this game goes. Do you understand? Now speak!"

"Yes." His voice was unsteady.

CRACK!!! She swung the whip.

"That's yes *ma'am*! Now have you ever ate pussy before?"

"No ma'am." He frowned.

"Do you want to learn how?" she licked her lips.

"No ma'am!" he answered, uninterested in eating pussy.

"Oh! Yes, you do. Yeah you want to make me feel good, don't you? No is the wrong answer. Never fix your mouth to tell me no! Do you understand?" she spat.

"Yes ma'am." Tedrick responded.

"I know you do. Now… get your ass off that bed and come here." she ordered. He got up and started to walk over to where Blu'Jai was standing but got stopped dead in his tracks. "Crawl over here to your boss. Don't walk." she ordered.

Blu'Jai was by far the finest woman he had ever seen that wasn't on TV. The role play that they were having was such a turn on to him that he was willing to do whatever she said right about now. He crawled over to her and she ordered him to take off her thong.

"That's right." She wiggled a bit as Tedrick pulled her thong down "You like what you see?" she asked.

"Yes ma'am." he whispered.

"You want to make your controller feel good, don't you?" Blu'Jai asked as she rubbed the back of his head with her free hand, leading him where she wanted him.

"Yes ma'am." he smiled as he inhaled deeply and explored. Her love nest smelled like a bed of roses. She smelled delicious.

"That's a good boy! Fuck yeah! That's a good boy! I like that!" she said in a baby voice. "Lick that pussy Tedrick, lick your boss's pussy."

He stuck his tongue into the slit of her honey pot. Her lips were glazed with sticky honey, and her clitoris was erect.

"Oooh yes, that's a good boy. Put your tongue in it." she groaned, then let out a deep moan of sexual excitement as she ground against his face in slow motion.

She raised up her leg and ordered him to hold it up for her while she grabbed the back of his head to maintain her balance. Blu'Jai was in all out freak mode, and they were both driving each other wild.

"You like that pussy, don't you?" she moaned as she thrust her love box into his mouth with so much force you could see the dimples in her booty cheeks. "It's not so bad huh?" it's not so bad ummmmm!"

Blu'Jai watched in amazement as Tedrick skillfully navigated through her love nest.

"Mmmhmm." Tedrick moaned when he heard Blu'Jai moan.

"You're such a good boy! You're making your boss feel SOOO good!!! Okay, put my leg down because you are about to stick that tongue in this ass." she said, turning around and putting one hand on the dresser and using the other hand to palm the back of his head as she guided it to the back of her thick ass.

"Be a good boy and lick this ass for your bitch." she commanded. As far as Blu'Jai was concerned, if you didn't eat her ass, you didn't fuck her right.

"Ohhhhh yeeaaah... good boooyyy..." she praised. "Put your face in that shit. Ummmm!!! Shit!!!Lick this ass boy!!! Put your whole face in it!!! You better not stop! You bet....ter....nooot! Fuuuuuck yesss!!!" Tedrick was enjoying his first oral experience when Blu'Jai pulled him to his feet and whispered, "my turn."

She grabbed his dick with both hands and pulled him to the other side of the room. After instructing him to sit up on the dresser, she went and grabbed a chair from the kitchen. When she returned, she spread his legs, placed the chair between them and sat down facing his dick. She then wrapped her full, plum-colored lips around his cock and gathered his ball sack in one of her palms. She was determined to tackle that big, long bad boy. Just the tip was damn near the back of her throat. She tried to fit a little more in her mouth and immediately started gagging. *Shit!* she thought. She took a deep breath, then slid the tip of his dick back into her mouth. She relaxed the back of her throat and moved her warm mouth up and down his dick. After she caught a rhythm and pace, then the shit was on. She tilted her head to the side a bit and sucked in her cheeks, so the sides of her jaws gave his dick an even snugger fit. No matter how hard she tried, his whole dick would not fit into her mouth. So she licked the remainder of his shaft from time to time to keep it wet, while she wrapped her hands around it to jack him off in her mouth. She had to use both hands, which was a first for her. But the head that she gave was fire and she was working with it.

Tedrick was in a state of shock and bliss at the same time. *Damn!* He thought to himself.

"Blu'Jai!" he screamed, but she didn't stop.

That well-oiled machine was working in overdrive. He shot his first load of happy juice in her mouth - which she swallowed with no hesitation - and to her delight, he was still hard.

Damn! I got me a young stud! she thought to herself as she pulled him to the bed by his dick. *And* his nut tasted delicious! She laid him on his back and got on top of him to ride reversed cowgirl style. She bounced her ass up and down on his big dick, slow at first, just to get used to the size of it. Then she worked that ass so good that they were both screaming each other's name to the hype of ecstasy.

Tedrick then got behind her to get some doggy style. The base of his dick was sliding and rubbing against her clitoris as he entered her again and again. Blu'Jai felt like he was about to knock her straight into the headboard, so she put one hand on it to prevent that from happening and the other hand on Tedrick's thigh to keep him from digging in her ass like that. She had never been fucked so thoroughly!

"Ooooh right there!" she screamed. "Ummmmmm!!! I'm cumming..." Blu'Jai cried and Tedrick shot a huge load of his nut inside of her. "Damn, that was good!" Blu'Jai smiled and playfully punched him in the chest.

Tedrick was speechless.

"You want some orange juice before round two?" she teased, getting out of the bed with her ass jiggling everywhere.

"Yeah. Sure." Tedrick replied, laying back with his hands behind his head. He was so glad that they had met. And it was official: *Ayanna is history,* he thought to himself.

Blu'Jai walked back in the room and handed him a tall glass of OJ and sat hers on the nightstand. She grabbed her robe, slipped it on and headed back to the front.

"Where you going?" Tedrick asked.

"Someone is knocking on the door."

He frowned.

"That's what I'm saying!" I hate for folks to show up unannounced, fucking up my groove and shit! I'll be right back, okay?"

"Okay," he said.

Blu'Jai left back out the room and went towards the front door. Whoever it was on the other side of the door continued to knock - more like beating on the door anxiously for it to be answered. She went to the door, looked through the tiny peephole and saw an older woman which whom she didn't recognize.

"Who is it?"

"Miss Moss."

Miss Moss?? Neither her name nor face didn't rang a bell. But she didn't want to be rude, so she opened the door.

"May I help you?" Blu'Jai asked, holding her robe together.

"Yes. I am looking for my son Tedrick,"

Oh Shit! Blu'Jai thought.

"Yes, he is over here." Blu'Jai said as the woman eyed her standing there half naked.

"May I please come in? I need to speak with you." Miss Moss asked.

"Sure, come on in." Blu'Jai opened the door all the way up allowing her entrance.

"Where is my son?" she questioned.

"I'll go get him." Blu'Jai said, turning to inform Tedrick that his mother was in the living room.

"Tedrick!" Blu'Jai stated.

"Mama!" Tedrick screamed as he tried to pull the sheets on the bed over his naked body.

Blu'Jai didn't know Miss Moss had followed her into the room. Miss Moss took in the scene and a picture popped in her mind of what might have just happened. She saw the red thong on the floor, the whip, the black stripper boots…and her eighteen-year-old son naked in the bed of a grown ass woman that looked to be the closer to her age than her son's.

"The fuck? Tedrick! Get yo ass up, put yo clothes on and let's go!" Miss Moss yelled. "Bitch, I'm hip to your games. You should be ashamed."

"I'm not." Blu'Jai stated flatly and unmoved.

"You groupie ass bitch! Stay the fuck away from my son before I fuck you up! Ayanna called me and told me all about the games you're running. She said you got him driving your car and shit! How fucking irresponsible is that. This boy don't even have a driver's license! And you at a damn high school Halloween party with your ass hanging all out! You ought to be ashamed of your fucking self! Ayanna wants to whip your ass, and right about now I do too! Leave my son alone and find you another sucker to try to use, because he won't be the one!"

Blu'Jai allowed Miss Moss to vent without a comment of her own. She deliberately let her robe fall open, because she wanted to confirm the fact that she and Tedrick had indeed just had a sexual encounter. It was a personal, unspoken victory that she was celebrating in front of Miss Moss. She grinned and listened to Tedrick's mother carry on, not giving a piece of damn about one word she was saying. She knew in her heart that none of what his mother was saying even mattered, because after the good pussy she had just given him, he wouldn't be able to stay away. Good pussy was power.

Tedrick finished getting dressed and followed his mother out the door with his head down not saying a word. So, she just locked the door and went to bed with a knowing smile on her face.

CHAPTER 9

I do not give up!

Two weeks had passed, and Blu'Jai hadn't heard a word from Tedrick. He had stopped coming over in the mornings, and basically had cut off all forms of communication with her. This was a first for Blu'Jai. There had never been a man – or boy - that she has slept with who she didn't have to damn near get rid of afterwards. Men always became obsessed after she blessed them with her goods. *So why was his young ass able to resist?* she wondered. The only answer that she could seem to come up with was his mother,

I've got to find a way around that bitch, Blu'Jai said to herself as she sat on her couch watching old reruns of *Martin*. She had always thought Martin was so cute; and she hated that Thomas Mikal Ford, AKA "Tommy," had passed.

She sat crossing her legs under her behind grabbing her cellphone she called Kyron and was sent straight to voicemail.

"Hoe ass nigga!" she spat into the recording. "I should pull up on yo ass for playing me!" She hung up and made another call.

"Hey! Were you busy?" she asked Coach Griffen when he answered.

"Not for you! How are you? I haven't seen you in a while, and your phone always goes straight to voicemail when I call" He sounded happy to hear from her.

"Been kinda under the weather, but I'm good. I was just wondering if you wanted to get together?"

"Sure!" he quickly answered. "We've got to play the State Championship game this Saturday in Austin though."

"Oh! Really! You guys made it to the State Championship? That's great!"

"Yeah! We went undefeated this year, and with Tedrick coming back, I see another undefeated year in the horizon. That kid has thrown and ran for a combined thirty-two touchdowns this year. One more will break a record for the most touchdowns with no interceptions by a quarterback. He will break that record Saturday and go down in the history books. Why don't you come with us? I mean, we're staying the night at the Comfort Inn. It's not too expensive, but it's nice… and you could be my roommate."

"Sounds like a plan." she said.

"I'm going to ride the bus with the guys, but you can drive my Lexus, then maybe we can grab a bite to eat. On Friday, everyone's going to hang out at the pool to kinda relax and celebrate, so be sure to bring your swimsuit. It's a heated indoor pool."

"Okay. So when can I pick up the car?"

"Well I was thinking of dropping by after practice, hanging out with you for a while, then you can take me home and just keep the car so you can leave for Austin whenever you want tomorrow."

"I'll be here waiting." She said flirtatiously.

To be an athletic trainer, Coach Griffen didn't have the stamina Blu'Jai was expecting. He came by her place and within an hour they had fucked, filled up his car, and dropped him off at home. One hour! She took longer than that to wash her ass. *Either my shit just too good, or he just too sad,* she thought to herself.

Prolly a mixture of both.

$ $ $ $ $

Blu'Jai threw her overnight bag into the backseat of Coach Griffen's Lex and hit the highway. It was a three-and-a-half-hour trip from Dallas to Austin, so she just set the cruise control and coasted all the way there. She arrived and got the key to the room at the Comfort Inn, which was under coach Griffin's and her name. He had sent her the money for the incidentals to her Cash App. Blu had beat the team there, and that was a good look for her, because she could go grab a quick shower, and then a nap. The room was nice and comfortable. She jumped into the hot shower, dried off with the big fluffy bath towel, and sprayed on some of her favorite YSL perfume. She climbed into the bed and quickly dozed off. A few hours later, she was awakened by a stinging slap on her ass cheek. She hadn't bothered to put on any clothes or crawl under the covers before she napped. She was an expert in the art of seduction, and she knew the sight of her plump, naked ass exposed in the bed while she was sleeping would be a terrific first sight for ANY man walking into a hotel room.

"Hey Coach, you made it?" Blu'Jai asked sleepily in a soft voice as she rubbed the spot on her ass that he had just popped.

"Yeah, we been here. I was just making sure the boys got into their rooms okay. So, there was no need to wake you. Shit, you looked so good laying there I almost said *fuck the boys* and let them find their rooms on their own."

"You did the right thing." she said, laughing.

"You didn't have any problems getting, here did you?" the coach asked while taking off his Nikes.

"Not at all. The Lex rides great, but not quite as good as me." She said with a wicked grin, then patted on the bed with two quick taps. "Come here Coach."

He started to unzip his shorts.

"That won't be necessary. Just lay down on your back." she instructed.

Blu'Jai wasn't in the mood for any sorry dick. Good dick was one thing, but Coach Griffen didn't fit that bill. She climbed on top of his face and kissed his lips with her pussy lips. She was in the mood for a quick nut, just like he always got from her. So, this time the shoe was on the other foot, she thought as she began to grind her pussy into his face.

"Damn Coach!" she moaned as he licked her clit.

If he wasn't good at anything else, he could damn sure eat some pussy. She bounced on his face until she filled his mouth with her nectar. Damn you do it so good…." she purred as she climbed off him.

"Glad you enjoyed it. I guess we can finish what we started later. Everyone's about to go to the pool right now because I gave them a strict ten o'clock curfew. So throw on your swimsuit if you brought one, and I'm about to put on my trunks."

Blu'Jai put on a black two-piece Dolce & Gabbana bikini, and a pair of DKNY peekaboo high heeled sandals. She'd picked that bikini hoping to get Tedrick's attention when she saw him, and he saw her. She had to get him to see shit her way. She had to steal his heart away from those other bitches that had a hold of it. He was her winning lotto ticket, and she was about to lose it. In fact, to her the game was only the beginning. Folks always said that the key to a man's heart was through his stomach, but to Blu'Jai, that theory was outdated and irrelevant.

Shiiit... the key to a nigga's heart is through his dick! Blu'Jai said to herself. That theory had been tested and proven repeatedly.

Coach put on a pair of Polo trunks and flip flops, then they headed to the pool. Someone had brought their iPod and hooked it to some speakers. It was like a pool party out there. The cheerleaders, drill team, band, and the football team were all out there swimming - splashing water and having water gun fights. Some of the guys had girls on their shoulders in the water, and the girls were trying to push the other girls off. That's when Blu'Jai spotted Tedrick. Ayanna was on his neck and they were laughing, having a good time in the water.

Blu'Jai's booty jiggled like jelly as she walked around the pool. A few of the parents and the booster club members were dancing to a song by Cardi B that was playing through the speakers.

"Come on," Coach said grabbing her hand and pulling her towards the dancing group. "Show these kids how it's done!" he continued.

Blu'Jai didn't want to get raunchy, although she could give a stripper a run for their money. She kept it smooth and sexy. She had managed to make eye contact with Tedrick, and that gave her all the motivation she needed. She turned her ass so that he could have the best view in the house and started a slow wind. Her moves were sensual and very enticing as she slowly bounced her ass from side to side. She arched her back a little and smiled to herself knowing Tedrick's eyes were probably glued to her jiggling ass. After she felt that she had made her presence known to her satisfaction she cut her show short. She made sure Tedrick was watching as she leaned in and whispered into the Coach's ear.

"I'm about to go back to the room. Don't be all night out here. Remember, we have some unfinished business."

The smile on Coach Griffen's face left no doubt in Tedrick's mind that the secret words that were just shared between them were of a sexual nature, and the sight of Coach Griffen's hand resting on her ass only enraged him more. Blu'Jai glanced at Tedrick and saw all that she needed to see. He was pissed, so she added fuel to the fire and blew him a discreet kiss before strutting like a super model on a runway back to their room.

"What is she doing here?" Ayanna asked Tedrick. She had watched the whole scene and didn't miss anything, not even that tired old school move Blu'Jai made by blowing Tedrick a kiss.

"I think she's here with coach." he answered.

"Good!" Ayanna mumbled.

"I may not have to kill yo ass! She's so damn nasty, out here in that shit, bikini all up in the crack of her ass! I swear I could just beat her ass!"

Ayanna despised Blu'Jai and Blu'Jai knew it, but she didn't give a lovely fuck. Ayanna had something that she wanted and that belonged to her. A guaranteed life of the rich and famous. Blu'Jai's mind was working overtime but she was glad that she made the trip. She pulled a pair of sweats out her bag, tied a scarf around her head and put on a pair of thick white socks. She didn't feel like dealing with Coach Griffen anymore tonight. She'd hope that he would come to the room and go to sleep. She had bigger fish to fry, and she had already accomplished a big part of her mission.

By the time Coach made it up to the room, he decided that he needed to rest as well. He was pumped about the game, so he went over the game plays that he had on his tablet and called it a night.

Blu'Jai woke up to an empty bed, which was fine by her. She checked her messages on her phone and there was a text from Coach:

I left fifty dollars under your night bag. I hope that you don't mind eating breakfast alone. I had to go eat with the team. I won't be back to the room, but I'll see you at the game.

The game was at noon so Blu'Jai figured she'd better start getting ready since it was already ten. She texted the words, *Thank you and good luck!*' to Coach, then started fixing her hair. She put on a short skin-tight Tameca's Denym & Diamonds dress and a pair of thong heeled sandals. She looked in the mirror at herself and liked what she saw. She knew she was overdressed for a high school football game, but what the hell. This dress hugged her ass perfectly and her booty was an instant magnet to men in this dress. She jumped into Coach's Lexus and stopped at Denny's restaurant. She ordered a Grand Slam breakfast, and the young black female waitress eyed her before she whispered, "This is on the house. Call me sometimes." she said, laying a card on the table with her number next to a plate of bacon, eggs and waffles. Blu'Jai smiled and stuck the card in her bosom knowing that she would never use it. However, the waitress only confirmed that she had on the right outfit.

She arrived at the stadium about fifteen minutes before kickoff. She quickly parked and presented the ticket Coach had given her to the gate attendant. The crowd was amped and hyped for the game. Everywhere Blu'Jai looked, she saw Carter Cowboy t-shirts with Tedrick's picture on it. She couldn't believe her eyes. It was like he was already famous; he just didn't have the money. People even had homemade signs with Tedrick's picture on it that read, "T-Moss for President!" As she was making her way to the seats out of all the people she could have bumped into, she bumped into Miss Moss. She also had a T-Moss shirt on with his number eight on her chest. Miss Moss looked Blu'Jai up and down and shook her head in disgust.

"Hood Rat!" she mumbled before walking off.

Blu'Jai shot her a finger behind her back. *Bitch better quit playing with me before she gets her old ass whipped,* Blu'Jai said to herself.

Blu'Jai bought a set of pompoms and a T-Moss #8 hat from a lady that had a table full of T-Moss memorabilia. The ball cap didn't match her dress, but she couldn't let all these nobody's rep Tedrick like that without her representing him as well while she sat back trying to look cute. She cocked her hat on her head, careful not to fuck her hair up, and found a seat just as Tedrick lead his team onto the field. The crowd went crazy as Tedrick pumped his fist and pointed to the sky. Blu'Jai stood up, waved her pom-poms and shouted along with the rest of them.

"Woooo!!!" she screamed as she watched Tedrick slap his wide receiver's helmet.

Chapter 10

Winners are not people who never fail, but people who never quit.

The game was getting ready to start and the Cowboys were on the field and ready to play. This was going to be one of the best games of the Carter Cowboys' history.

"You ready?!!!" Tedrick screamed in the face of his All-American receiver as he slapped the side of his helmet.

"I'm ready!!! You ready?!!!" he screamed as they traded slaps on the helmets back and forth, before jumping high into the air and chest-bummping.

"Let's go then!!!" Tedrick screamed, nodding his head up and down repeatedly. He was ready! It was on!

"Huuddllle!!!" Coach Griffen yelled, and all the guys and coaches grouped close together.

"Who are we?" Tedrick screamed in the middle of the pack, looking around to find the eyes of each and every one of his soldiers that were ready to battle side with him on that field today.

"Cowboys!!!" everyone answered in unison.

"Who are we?!"

"Cowboys!!!"

"Who are we?"

"Cowboys!!!"

"We're the Carter Cowboys!" Tedrick pumped, then looked in the direction of the opposing team with a scowl on his face. This was war.

"We operate as one unit! I need you, and you need me! We've come a long way, but today we still have work to do guys! Y'all are my brothers on that field, and that means I'm going to kick, bite, and scratch out there for you. It's us against them. And whoever wants it most will take what's ours, and that's the victory! Y'all with me?!!"

"Hell Yeah!!!" they screamed after Tedrick's pep talk and they all took a knee and Coach Griffen said a prayer with all heads bowed.

Since the championship game was the last game of the year, all the seniors were team captains. This was the only time Tedrick hadn't walked out on the field for the coin toss. He'd always been captain on every team he'd ever played on. He turned around to scan the stands to find his mother, so he'd know where she was sitting, just like he did before every game. That's when he saw Blu'Jai waving her pom-poms with his game hat on her head. She was bouncing up and down and her titties looked like they were about to pop out the little dress she was wearing. *Good luck!* She mouthed to him and winked. He had to admit that he missed the fuck out of her. She was looking good as hell to him, and always seemed to find a way to stand out from everyone else. He gave her thumbs up, and just that small gesture melted her heart. Then Tedrick noticed Coach Griffen waved to her as well, and at that very moment Tedrick wanted to hit his coach in the mouth. *Fuck her!* he said to himself, and continued to scan the crowded stands until he spotted his mom.

"Okay Moss, we've got the ball first!" Coach Griffen said, but Tedrick's mind was on fucking his coach up, so everything he was being told went into one ear and out the other.

"Take care of the ball like you've been doing, and these boys don't stand a chance!" Coach continued.

Tedrick ran onto the field after the kickoff and huddled his team. He got the play from Coach and brought the team up to the line of scrimmage. He hiked the ball and tried to pitch it to the runningback's hand. It was like the guy wasn't even looking for the ball and before Tedrick could jump on the ball to recover it, the defense had scooped up the ball and rumbled down the field into the end-zone. The first play of the game the score was six to zero, and thirty seconds hadn't even come off the clock.

"What the hell was that Moss?!" Coach screamed as Tedrick ran to the sideline with his mind stuck on Blu'Jai.

"Sean didn't catch the ball!!" he said.

"That's cuz it was a fuckin' pass play! He wasn't even supposed to get the damn ball! I called a gotdamn pass play! Get your head in the game kid!" Coach scolded then slapped him on his ass to let Tedrick know shit happens, but they would be okay.

Tedrick got the play after the next kick off and took the offense back out on the field. He hiked the ball and dropped back to pass and immediately got sacked. The next play, he dropped back to pass the ball to his wide receiver, but the pass was intercepted. Tedrick ran after the guy who intercepted the ball and laid a booming hit on him. The guy jumped right up celebrating his interception, but Tedrick laid on the field motionless. Coach Griffen, as well as the rest of the coaching staff, ran out on the field to tend to their superstar quarterback. Blu'Jai said a silent prayer for Tedrick:

God please don't let him be hurt bad. If he can't play football, I don't know what I'm going to do!

A small John Deer cart rolled out onto the field and they laid Tedrick on the back of it. The crowd was silent, and players on both teams were down on one knee. Some saying prayers, others shaking their heads in disbelief. Tedrick gave the crowd a thumbs up and fans on both teams applauded. Tedrick's teammates ran up to the cart and slapped his helmet as they took him away to the locker room. Coach Griffen ran beside the cart worried to death about his superstar's condition. Blu'Jai made her way out of the stands and walked down to the locker room entrance, but an armed police officer wouldn't let her through. A few minutes later, Coach Griffen emerged through the door.

"How is he?" Blu'Jai asked.

"We think it's a sprained ankle, I don't think he's going to be able to finish the game. He's pretty upset."

"Can I go in to see him?"

"Yeah go ahead." Coach said.

"You can let her in," he told the officer.

The officer nodded and held the door open for Blu'Jai, and Coach hurried back to the sideline with the rest of his team. Blu'Jai looked in a couple rooms before she found Tedrick. He had already taken his shoulder pads off, and the last trainer was leaving to head back out to the field.

"How are you feeling?" she asked. That was the first time Blu'Jai had seen Tedrick's head hung so low.

"Fuck you! What are you doing here?" he turned his head to avoid looking at her.

"I came to check on you. I just came to check on you," she said softly.

"I think you need to check on coach, bitch!" he spat.

"You watch your fucking mouth! You don't talk to me like that! I'm tired of playing with you Tedrick!"

"Well what are you going to do about it?" he screamed. The pain in his heart was just as sharp as the pain in his ankle.

"You're fucking coach!" he snatched up his helmet and slung it across the locker room.

"Stop it! The only reason I came here was to see you! You act like you couldn't call or come by my house after your mother told you not to! You're the one acting like a fuckin' kid. A fuckin' little boy that must do what his mommy says do and can't make choices like a man! Then you still screwing with what that lil bitch Anita!" Her hands were on her hips.

"It's Ayanna!" Tedrick corrected.

"Yeah! What the fuck ever! Look Tedrick, baby! I want you and I know you want me, so let's stop with these games and just do us," she pleaded.

Blu'Jai paused and stared at Tedrick. She saw the wheels turning in is head and the thump of his heart beneath his sweaty t-shirt.

"Fuck what anyone thinks, it can just be you and me! I don't want coach. Trust me!" She spread her arms and showed her palms to him.

"What about mom and Ayanna?" His voice was low.

"I'm not trying to disrespect your mom, but fuck them! When you get home, you get your shit and move in with me!" Blu'Jai knew she had him if she just kept pushing.

"You serious?" he finally asked after a long pause.

"Hell yes! Now are you going to be able to go back out there? That other team is beating us like stepchildren," she asked, kneeling beside him rubbing his ankle.

"My ankle hurts like hell!" he frowned.

"Let me give you something to take your mind off the pain." she said with a sly grin.

In her mind, pussy could heal the world. She laid him back on the bench he was sitting on and started undoing his pants.

"What are you doing? Someone may walk in here and catch us." Tedrick didn't want to jeopardize his position.

"Okay, I'm going to need you to stop being so damn scary! You are going to have to start manning up baby!" she said, licking her lips and paying his request for her to stop no mind as she continued to fidget with his pants. She pulled his pants down and gasped in pure delight, at the sight of his long hard dick that was nestled snuggly in his jock strap. "Looks like he missed mama too!" she said, looking into his eyes.

"I'm going to fix that. He won't ever miss mama again." she said as she slipped his dick out the side of his jock strap.

She pulled up her dress over her hips revealing her voluptuous ass. She took her index finger, dug her thong out her crack, and pulled it to the side.

"Now follow the bouncing booty." she instructed in her baby voice as she turned around, grabbed his dick, and guided it into her wet pussy.

She slid down the length of his pole and rested her ass cheeks on his torso. She spread his legs wide as she could, then placed a hand on each of his knees.

"You ready for this ride T-Moss?" she teased, looking back at him over her shoulder. "Yeah, I know you ready," she said as she started picking her ass up and twerking like she had Megan Thee Stallion's knees.

She bounced up and down and started picking up speed. She looked back over her shoulder again and almost came herself when she saw the expression on his face. He was all frowned up with mouth cocked half open and eyes closed. Her mouth formed an O shape and wrinkles appeared in her forehead. She clenched her teeth then managed to find her voice.

"I said follow the bouncing bo-boootyyy. Open your eyes and watch mama work this assss." Blu'Jai said as she gained more speed.

"Watch it T-Moss, it does tricks!" she moaned as she started grinding her ass when picking it up then rocking it from side to side and dropping it back down.

She gripped his pole with her pussy muscles when she came up and rocked the boat when she brought it back down.

"It looks like the pussy is just eating that dick don't it?" She said as she rode him like a certified pro. "Cum in this pussy T-Moss! Cuuum in this ass! Oooh yeah! Hell yea! Quarterback this shit. I'm about to cuuummm! Fuck yeah! Quarterback this shit! Ummmmmm! Ummhmm…you came all in this pussy!"

She hopped off quickly, sucked the residue off his dick, and stuck it back into his jock strap. She kissed him and stuck her tongue in his mouth.

"I really want you to try to go back out there and play." she whispered, looking him in his eyes. "Can't the trainers wrap it up and you try to give it a go since this is the last game? Plus, I heard it's a lot of scouts out there."

"I guess I could try." he said as he looked Blu'Jai in her eyes. He was ready to do anything she asked.

"Try for me," she begged as she stood up, pulled her dress back down and picked up her pompoms up off the ground.

"Oh, and ummm... don't you ever forget who the boss is again." She eyed him seriously and he nodded. "You're mine now, so I call the shots in your regard from this point on." Blu'Jai made herself clear.

"Send a trainer in here to wrap it up for me," Tedrick said as he sat up and rubbed his ankle.

"Okay. I'll go get one right now!" she said excitedly as her heels clicked clacked against the concrete as she walked out the locker room. Her walk bolstered confidence. She suddenly stopped and turned around. "I meant what I said. I was playing when we role played, but things are too crucial right now, so you gone obey me, and only me Tedrick," she warned like a mother says to her child with a raised brow.

Blu'Jai was greeted at the door by an agitated Miss Moss.

"What is the skeezer doing in here?" she asked the officer who was standing at the entrance.

"Why don't you talk to me like a woman!?" Blu'Jai said, coming to an abrupt stop standing directly in front of Miss Moss. "There's no need to act ghetto all the damn time."

She threw her hands on her hips, sucked her teeth and rolled her neck. Blu'Jai was vibing on a whole other level right now. She was winning, and really didn't have time for Tedrick's goofy ass mother.

"I've been trying to show you respect, but you are really pushing it!"

Miss Moss wasn't one to back down from a fight, so she quickly snatched off her earrings. "I told this bitch that I was going to kick her ass if she didn't stay away from my son!" she said to the officer as if she was looking for permission to succeed.

"You two ladies can't be out here fighting, so just calm down," he said clearly amused by what he was seeing.

"Look Miss Moss, like it or not, Tedrick isn't a baby anymore! He's a grown man, and trust me I'm very sure of that!" she stated with a raised brow. "I'm sure you know that my word is credible." she continued, giving Miss Moss a flashback of her son laid up in her bed the night she busted into her bedroom.

"He's not just a grown man, he's my man! You've done a great job with raising him, but I'm going to take it from here. I'm going to take good care of Tedrick, so you don't have to worry. And one more thing: if you can manage to find a smile, keep it on your face and act civilized. I may allow you to stay in his good graces! Now if you'll excuse me, I've got a game to go watch!" Blu'Jai said then shook her pompoms with a smile on her face before walking off.

Miss Moss had an astonished look on her face and her mouth dropped wide open, but she couldn't find her voice. She reached out in attempt to snatch Blu'Jai's ass up by the back of her long bundles, but the officer grabbed her up by her waist to stop her. Her legs kicked out in the air a few times as she attempted to escape his strong grasp.

"Put me down, I need to go check on my son!" she screamed.

The officer turned her loose, she straightened up her clothes, then went in to see Tedrick. Tedrick was strapping his shoulder pads back on when she walked in.

"Hey mama. What's up?" he said in a weak voice and looked away from his mother's intense gaze.

"What are you doing? I was told that you couldn't get back on the field without the risk of further injuring your ankle." She was worried about her son's future, even if it meant canning today's game.

"Yeah, I know, but I want to play so I'm going to get it taped up really good."

"Teddy, look at me." his mother said in a sincere tone.

His gaze met hers and what she saw made a tear fall from her eye. She was very familiar with that look; it was a look of a man in love.

"Son. Did she tell you to play?" Regina shook her head in disbelief.

"Well, yeah. She said she thinks I should."

"Son! That woman ain't no good! Please son! She doesn't give a damn about you. All she sees is dollar signs! She's taking advantage of your youthful mind. And I'm not by any means trying to take a shot at your growth as a man, but that woman is very manipulative. Don't fall into her trap and go back into that game, it's dangerous. You could ruin your ankle for good and it could cause you to not play next season. It's not even that important. Ayanna said to tell you she loves you."

Suddenly the locker room was filled with noise and sweaty teenaged football players. It was halftime, and they all had solemn looks on their faces.

"I'm about to leave so y'all can do whatever it is that y'all do at halftime. I love you son." She finished, kissing him on the forehead.

Miss Moss walked out of the locker room and glanced at the scoreboard; the score was fourteen to zero. Damn! She said to herself, clearly disappointed that Carter was about to take their first loss of the season. She made her way back to her seat, where some of the other parents questioned her about her son's status. She informed them that he wouldn't be returning to the game to play, and everyone had looks of disappointment.

After halftime was up, the teams emerged from the locker rooms and the bands exited the field after dancing and entertaining the crowd. Miss Moss was pleased to see that Tedrick had followed her advice when she didn't see him in the pack with his teammates as they took the field. The Cowboys were on defense to start the second half, and they held the Knights' offense to just three plays before making them kick the ball away, which was the first time the whole game they had done that. Their defensive stand caused the crowd to come back to life. The stadium starting rocking and everyone was suddenly on their feet. Miss Moss had never heard a crowd get so pumped over one defensive stop, but suddenly she realized what all the commotion was about; it was because she saw Tedrick and a trainer running out of the locker room towards the sideline. The school band started playing Da Baby's "Suge." The cheerleaders were jumping up and down, doing splits and toe touches high in the air. The crowd started chanting, "Teee Mooosss! Teee Mooosss! Teee Mooosss!"

The helmet in Tedrick's hand bounced against his thigh as his trainer jogged to join him with the team. His trainer helped him strap his helmet on, and Tedrick's All-American receiver immediately ran over to greet him with a slap on the helmet.

"You ready!!!" he screamed as they traded slaps like they always did to hype each other up.

Coach Griffen's smile couldn't have been brighter. He knew that with Tedrick in the game they had a shot to make a dynamic comeback to win. Tedrick quickly scanned the crowd, but this time he was trying to avoid his mother's eyes. He was in search of Blu'Jai instead. When he spotted her, she mouthed the words *I Love You!* She smiled, bounced up and down and waved her pompoms. He pumped his fist and felt pretty good about himself as he got the play from his coach and ran out on the field.

Tedrick hiked the ball, dropped back to pass and spotted an open hole. He swiftly side stepped, then shot through the hole and dashed 76 yards into the end zone. The crowd went crazy as he and his teammates celebrated pulling within one score for the victory. The defense made another impressive stand, stripping the ball away from Kimball High's star running back, and now Tedrick was back on the field. Tedrick got the snap from his center and couldn't believe his eyes when he saw how open his wide receiver was! He licked his lips smelling victory. His receiver was the best in the nation as he was at quarterback, and he had sure hands. He cocked back to make a forty-yard throw down the field, then released the ball, and it was a perfect tight spiral pass. Everybody in the stadium was on their feet holding their breath as the ball sailed through the air. Suddenly a defender came out of nowhere making a basketball leap in the game, and snagged the ball out of the air. He made an unbelievable interception and sprinted back in the opposite direction with no time left on the clock. If he just would fall down the game would be over, but unfortunately the kid was a senior trying to impress the college scouts, so he flamboyantly held up the ball in the air to show the crowd he had it, then tried to return for a touchdown. Tedrick was pissed at his miscalculation on the pass. He sprinted with all his speed knowing there was no one between the guy and the end zone. Tedrick's speed was phenomenal; in fact, he was an All-American track star *and* quarterback. He dug deep and caught the guy, giving him a wicked blow that sent him crashing to the turf, violently knocking Tedrick out cold when his head hit the ground. He laid on the field unconscious for what seemed like an eternity. When his eyes finally opened, he was lying in a hospital bed.

"What's going on?" He asked in a weak voice as a doctor looked down at him.

"You suffered a bad concussion at the game an hour or so ago. We're going to keep you here to run a few tests on you. How do you feel?" The doctor asked.

"I'd feel a lot better if we had won the game today."

"You guys did win! I heard after you tackled the kid, the ball was fumbled and one of your teammates picked it up and ran all the way back for a touchdown. Everyone is talking about how heroic the play was today. I tell you, you're destined for greatness. Congratulations! But your mom wants to see you, so I'll give you a minute before we get started with the rest of the tests we need to run."

Miss Moss walked into her son's hospital room and smiled. "How are you feeling baby?"

"I'm good. Just sore all over, but I'll live."

"I hate that you didn't listen to me, but you played a hell of a game, son!" She smiled and softly punched his arm.

Tedrick held out his fist and she gave her son a pound.

"I brought Ayanna with me and she wants to see you. She's really upset because the skeezer is out there in the hallway too. Do you want me to tell that tramp to leave? I told her you probably didn't want to see her!"

"No mom, tell her to come in and tell Ayanna to leave," he frowned.

"What?" Miss Moss raised her voice.

"I want to see Blu'Jai," he said standing his ground.

"I can't believe this! That woman is the devil! She's the devil!" Miss Moss shook her head in disbelief.

"I want to see her! Fuck it! Blu'Jai!!!" He screamed loudly. "Blu'Jai!!!" He sang.

"Yeah honey, I'm here!" she said running into the room from the hallway.

"Bitch!!!" Miss Moss screamed then threw a punch at Blu'Jai which sailed by her face, but the second one she threw hit its target.

Blu'Jai and Miss Moss went at it like two pit bulls. Ayanna ran in the room and joined Miss Moss in the beat down of Blu'Jai. The doctor came in and called for security to come help break up the fight. They managed to pull the women apart, then asked Blu'Jai if she wanted to press charges.

"Hell-the-fuck yeah!" she screamed.

Tedrick watched his mama and Ayanna get handcuffed and read their rights before being taken off to jail.

"You see! "Miss Moss screamed "You see! I told you she's the devil. You're just going to let her send your mama to jail?! You haven't seen the last of me, Blu'Jai! I've got something for you since you can't leave my son alone. I'll see you in court bitch and get your ass for statutory rape! For fucking with my son! Now I'm damn sure going to teach your ass a lesson. So, you want to play hard ball?! I'm game! Now! When I get out of jail we will see who is going to hit the ball the hardest!"

"Blu'Jai," Tedrick pleaded. "Don't do this to my mom!"

"Shut up! You shut up, Tedrick! You saw the shit they just did to me and I'm tired of it. A day or two in jail will teach her ass a lesson," she said as the officers took them away.

"Never put a bitch in front of me. I don't give a shit if the bitch is your fuckin' mother! You hear me nigga!" Blu'Jai was pissed.

Coach Griffen came into the room to check on Tedrick. Blu'Jai informed him that she was going to be taking Tedrick home after he was released. They were thankful that the injury wasn't as severe as they originally thought. Tedrick was released after they were finished with all the tests they had ran, and Blu'Jai took him back to her apartment. He sat silently the whole ride to Blu'Jai's. The thought of his mother and Ayanna having to sit in jail had him nauseated. He felt like he'd betrayed the two women that had always been there for him, but he loved Blu'Jai.

Miss Moss made a call to Coach Griffen and informed him of the situation. She asked for his help and he didn't hesitate to post her bond. When she made bond, she was able to access her funds and reimburse Coach Griffen and pay for Ayanna's release as well. They were relieved to be headed back to Dallas. When they arrived home, the first thing Miss Moss noticed in her house was Tedrick's empty bedroom. She sobbed uncontrollably and Ayanna comforted her with a loving hug as she wiped her own tears.

CHAPTER 11

It's stages to these wages.

Tedrick and Blu'Jai enjoyed each other over summer break. She was teaching him new things, and surprisingly he was teaching her new things too. They would hit the gym every morning to work out after eating the breakfast she would make every morning. She would usually cut up fresh fruit, to avoid cooking anything fatty, which consisted of watermelon, apples, honeydew melon, cantaloupes, grapes and oranges.. He taught her about workouts that had her tummy tight and flat, and they would run at least five miles a day.

Before summer break was over, Blu'Jai found herself pregnant, which was fine by her. A child would ensure her a paycheck for the next eighteen years. Miles was still in jail and had started calling her out the blue. He asked if she would sell his Jaguar for him and give the money to his lawyer to appeal. He had received a five-year sentence for his assault on a police officer charge.

This nigga good and crazy, she thought. Niggas go to jail and expect a bitch he fucked over while he was free to forgive, forget and hold him down! How stupid can these assholes be? She decided to give the car to Tedrick because she sure as hell wasn't gonna give Dickhead Miles one red cent. She thought about texting Natural, but dismissed the thought just as quickly as it entered her mind.

$ $ $ $ $

Summer break was over, and it was time for Tedrick to go back to school for his last year. Tedrick pulled up in the school parking lot in the cream colored XJ Jaguar on the first day. He thought he was the shit in the flashy luxury car, and he really was. He was flamboyant with a cock sure attitude. He had gained muscle without losing any of his speed, and Blu'Jai had paid for him to go to an NFL quarterback camp where he trained with several NFL quarterbacks. So, his game was on a whole other level, and he knew it.

Football season started and Tedrick led his team to another undefeated year, and another football state championship. He had accumulated more wins than any other quarterback in Carter High School history. Blu'Jai never missed a game. She cheered him on every step of the way.

She went into labor two months later, and gave birth to a baby girl named Kyler. Tedrick was disappointed that his mother didn't show up for the birth of his baby girl, her granddaughter. Miss Moss hadn't had any contact since getting out of jail, and Blu'Jai was way past fine with that. However, they were both oblivious that Miss Moss was still contemplating filing a statutory rape charge.

He was rocked to the core that she didn't come to one single game that year, and it was tough for Tedrick not seeing her there. She hadn't missed a game for the entire time he played football. She had been there for his little league, junior high and high school games. Rain, sleet or snow, she was there. His mother would be there even if his teammates' parents opted to stay home. But now Blu'Jai was his number one fan, and he was hers.

Tedrick kissed his precious daughter on her forehead and thought to himself, if only my mother could understand that I am happy, and happier than I have ever been in my life.

Back at home from the hospital, hours after being released, Blu'Jai said to Tedrick, "I need to talk to you honey." as she carefully eased down on the bed next to him while holding Kyler.

"What's up ,beautiful?"

She took a deep breath and swallowed. "Well I've been talking to this guy, he's a representative for Texas University."

"I'm already committed to TCU." Tedrick interrupted.

"Verbally! You haven't signed anything! But anyway, I've been talking to him and he has offered to give us five-hundred thousand dollars for you to play for Texas."

Tedrick rolled his eyes up in the air looking at the ceiling saying, "Nope! Blu'Jai, I can't do that! You know that I can't get caught in that kind of scandal. It would ruin my college career!"

"Look baby, we have a child now to think about and take care of! Think about your little girl! Do you want her to go without?

I told him that I would talk to you about it, if he paid for that NFL quarterback camp you went to this summer."

Tedrick jumped up off the bed and he was furious. "What?!!! I thought you paid for that!" he panicked.

"Where the hell was I gonna get that kind of money? Three-thousand dollars is a lot of money, and money I don't have Tedrick! Where do you think the money is coming from around here when neither of us have a job? How the fuck is the rent being paid, food in the icebox, pampers for your daughter's ass and clothes on your ass!" Blu'Jai said.

"Wow! So, are you telling me, you've been taking money from a sponsor?" he screamed.

"Hell yeah! What the fuck else was I supposed to do? When we all need shit around here!!!"

Tedrick was getting angrier by the minute. "I'm about to go!" he yelled, laying Kyler on the bed and grabbing his car keys.

"Where in the hell do you think you're going?" she said.

"Away from here, before I do something I'll regret!" he said.

"Like what? Tedrick!" she screamed pushing his shoulder. "What the fuck are you going to do, Mr. Perfect! Everyone does this Tedrick, why are you tripping? Texas is a much better school anyway! Me and Kyler will move to Austin with you. Just…just do this, baby. Have I ever told you to do anything that led to a bad result? Haven't I always taken care of you even when your own mother turned her back on you?"

Tedrick dropped his head at the mentioning of his mother. Blu'Jai wrapped her arms around his neck and pulled his head into her bosom.

"You know mommy is not going to let anything happen to you," she said in a soft baby voice.

He wrapped his arms around her waist, and she knew she had him, it was time to go for the kill.

"I already have the five-hundred-thousand-dollar check and a Texas University scout will be at your school on Senior Signing Day, the news and the works. Plus, you know I'll be there looking good." Blu'Jai promised.

"What do you mean you already have the money? I haven't signed a letter of intent."

"I was just sure you would see things my way. You always do, baby. I've already got us a nice townhouse in Austin with some very nice furniture. Everything is set and all you have to do is sign. I told you mommy was going to take care of everything. So, what do you say, because you know we can't pay this money back?"

"I guess I'm going to be a Texas Longhorn." he answered, knowing he was making a big mistake. But they already had the money, so his hand had been forced.

Blu'Jai traded in the Nissan Altima and got a champagne colored Infiniti. She basically lived in Neiman Marcus and the PRADA shop at the Galleria Dallas. She bought herself everything from Fendi, Chanel, to Versace and Louis Vuitton. This was how shit was supposed to be for her. She always knew that she was destined to have the finer things in life.

It was the end of Tedrick's high school year, and it was prom night. Tedrick was dressed immaculate in his thirteen-hundred-dollar, three button pinstriped Polo suit by Ralph Lauren. He had on Murphy Greenwich wingtip shoes, a French Regent shirt with the English Rapp striped tie and he topped the ensemble off top with some Himalaya Natural spray by Creed.

"Come on Blu baby!" he yelled from the living room as he glanced at the Tag Heuer watch Blu'Jai had just bought him.

"I'm coming." She had a look of radiance when she came out of the bedroom. Latoya Logan did Blu'Jai's hair in a long ponytail that hung over her left shoulder.

"How do I look honey?" she asked seductively.

"Flawless!" he answered unable to take his eyes off her.

Blu'Jai was wearing a black strapless Gucci dress that hugged her body like a glove and stopped only inches below her stupendous ass. Her skin was gleaming, and she had on Tom Ford heels, and Michael Kors designer frames. Her juicy lip gloss, and the intoxicating smell of Daylight spray by Ralph Lauren was absolutely intoxicating.

This was indeed a special night for Tedrick. To top it off, he was back on speaking terms with his mother. Tedrick had built up the nerve to call and speak to his mom weeks earlier, to apologize and to inform her about her granddaughter. His mother was happy to hear from him. He was her only child, and she had a granddaughter now. She wasn't about to miss out on being in her life, so she forgave her son. Tedrick asked his mom if she would babysit her granddaughter and Miss Moss said to him, without hesitation, "sure. I would be delighted to." This would be Kyler's first time spending the night with her grandmother, so neither one of them could wait.

On the way to the prom, Tedrick and Blu'Jai would drop Kyler at his mom's apartment, around the corner from where they lived. He pumped some 21 Savage out the speakers of the sparling new Infiniti. Blu'Jai wasn't big on rap music, but she didn't object since it was his day. When they arrived at his mom's place, Tedrick grabbed Kyler out of the car seat and knocked on his mom's door.

"Damn you are looking good boy!" Miss Moss screamed with a big smile on her face, happy to see her son.

"Thanks mom. It's good to see you!" he said leaning over to kiss her cheek as she snatched up her granddaughter.

"Look at granny's baby! She's as cute as can be!" she said kissing Kyler's face.

Kyler grinned in pure delight to be in her granny's arms. Tedrick handed her Kyler's diaper bag and was about to leave.

"Where's Blu'Jai?" his mother asked, shocking him that she had asked that question and didn't call her out her name.

"She's in the car waiting on me." he answered,

"Tell her to come here. I want to speak to her."

"Mom we really don't have time for that right now."

He didn't know what his mother had up her sleeve and he didn't want to find out, because he didn't want to ruin their night.

"Boy you ain't too grown to get your ass whooped. Now do what I told you to do and tell her to come here!"

"Yes ma'am." He said and walked to the car to tell Blu'Jai that his mom wanted to see her.

"What does she want with me?" she asked with a frown on her face. "I'm looking too cute to be out her fighting and shit Tedrick!" Blu'Jai's attitude was stank.

"Just come and see what she wants so we can leave."

He grabbed her hand and they walked holding hands towards the front door of his mother's apartment. She opened the door as soon as she saw them approaching.

"Y'all come on in." she said.

"Girl! Don't you look nice! How in the world is your stomach so flat after having Kyler? It took me damn near a year to lose mine after having this big head right here."

Blu'Jai looked dumbfounded by the way Miss Moss was acting. *This bitch acting like she's my bestie, like she aint been showing her ass and acting funny towards me for over a year. Is she serious?* she thought.

"Tedrick won't let me miss a day of working out and we don't eat any bread anymore." she said, trying to see where she was going with this.

"Let me get my iPhone so I can get a little video of you two. I know y'all about to leave me in a couple of weeks and have my Lil Kyler up in Austin."

"Miss Moss-"

"Call me Regina. And girl I like them glasses!"

"Well Regina…" Blu'Jai continued. "I want to apologize for disrespecting you. And thank you for learning to accept me, because I want the best for Tedrick just like you do."

"Blu'Jai you're family now. And it looks like you're going to be around if I like it or not, so I may as well get along with you, because being at each other's throat isn't healthy for anyone. I know I raised my son right and he's extremely intelligent, so I respect his decision-making. I just hope you can forgive me for being so protective of him. Now that you have a child of your own, you'll understand a mother's love. I just can't stand not being a part of y'all's life."

"I forgive you." Blu'Jai said and hugged Miss Moss for the first time.

Tedrick and Blu'Jai were headed out the door but before going out Tedrick said, "Mom we'll send you some videos of us."

She responded, "Good! I can't wait!" They headed to the senior prom a few minutes later.

"Your mom is really alright." Blu'Jai said.

"Yeah, she just gets a little crazy at times, but she means well."

Tedrick blasted the music as he pushed the luxury sedan down the freeway. He was jamming 21 Savage's "Bank Account." This song was one of the few that Blu'Jai liked.

"Heeeyyy, that's my shit!" Blu'Jai sang, then started snapping her fingers with both arms in the air as she swayed to the beat in the passenger seat.

"I got 1, 2, 3, 4, 5, 6, 7, 8 M's in my bank account..." Blu'Jai sang along.

Tedrick opened the sunroof and the stars were shining bright in the clear and dark black sky. Blu'Jai was excited to be attending her first prom - even if it was ten years after she'd missed her own.

At twenty-eight years old, she still felt like a kid at heart at, times and this was one of those times.

They arrived at the Rosewood Mansion on Turtle Creek in Dallas, and Tedrick handed the Valet a twenty-dollar bill after whispering in his ear. He grabbed Blu'Jai's hand and lead her into the upscale hotel. Marbled floors welcomed them, as well as a breathtaking crystal chandeliers. Blu'Jai strutted, switching her ample ass from side to side with a wide inviting smile on her face, fully aware that everyone in attendance knew her man was the bomb. She was a piece of eye candy that was sweet enough to send a diabetic into a coma. Coach Griffen gave a dramatic hand wave, but she quickly dismissed him, giving him an imperceptible nod. Ayanna was one of the first people Blu'Jai saw as they walked into the reception area where the prom was being held. She looked to have a handsome young man accompanying her as well, and Blu'Jai thought the little bitch was trying to be funny when she spoke to the two of them. Tedrick told her hello but Blu'Jai felt it would be demeaning to even acknowledge his ex. She wasn't even about to waste her breath, especially for this cow.

"Hi Tedrick, Hi Blu'Jai!!!" Blu'Jai repeated in Tedrick's ear mimicking Ayanna's voice sarcastically as they walked to their reserved table.

"I'm still lightweight mad about her jumping on me! Young ass bitch!"

"Blu, cool that shit out and let's enjoy this evening." Tedrick told her.

"Watch your mouth, mister.!" she said twirling a trio of thin diamond bracelets on her scrawny wrist.

"Don't make regret not bringing my whip!"

Enjoying themselves is just what they did. The meal was prepared by a top chef and the DJ pumped all the latest hits as they danced the night away. Just when Blu'Jai thought the night couldn't get any better, Tedrick told her that he had rented a suite with a mischievous grin.

"Heeeyyy!!!" she screamed as he led her to the elevator.

"Wowww!!! This is nice!" she exclaimed, taking in the marble vanities, mini bar, the silk pillows and throws.

She quickly wrapped her arms around his neck and ran her tongue around the inside of his mouth. His long possessive fingers squeezed her ass like it was an early Sunday morning. Her ass cheeks were oranges and they needed O.J.

"Wait," he said, breaking the lip lock. "I have a surprise for you," he said, excitedly grabbing the overnight bag off the sofa that he asked the bellboy to bring up for him when they arrived.

"Okay! But hurry up!" she said as she sat down on the couch and eagerly awaited him with her legs crossed.

Blu'Jai tried to collect herself and recapture her emotions when Tedrick's hand had emerged from the bag with a small expensive looking velvet box. He walked back over to her and bent down on one knee. He grabbed her left hand which was resting on her toned, ebony thigh. Blu'Jai dramatically clasped her right hand over her mouth when he opened the Tiffany & Co box. The size of the exquisite high-priced Tiffany Diamond ring made her stomach muscles tighten. Blu'Jai's eyes met with those of a young, tall, dark mocha complexed brother, that was undoubtedly in love. Blu'Jai flashed a smile that she had to learn from watching Tyra Banks for many years then squinted her eyes igniting her sex appeal.

"Desire and lust may affect one's judgement," Tedrick whispered. "But an ounce of prevention is better than a pound of cure. I'd be sick if I lost you. And even though I'm young, I'm willing to overcome my shortcomings as your man." Blu'Jai reached out and started to rub the back of his head.

"I've never been a loser but the last time I checked I hadn't been sporting any first place ribbons either in my relationships until I met you. We're about to leave Dallas in a few days to start a new life, and I really want to start it with you as my wife." Tedrick said as he grabbed Blu'Jai's hand and slid the humongous rock on her finger. His eye fell on her full breasts which were swelling.

"Tedrick, are you sure this is what you want?" she softly asked rubbing the back of her hand across the back of his face, with a light touch.

"I love you Blu."

"Let me see if you're ready for this." She said as she pulled Tedrick to his feet and led him to the king-sized bed. She laid him down then walked over to turn on the stereo.

Blu'Jai was addicted to role play, and she hated she didn't have a costume to put on. She found a station that was playing some hip-hop, knowing it was Tedrick's preference. She then climbed into the bed, high heels and all, and stood in the center. She seductively danced and squeezed her large titties together.

"You sure this is what you want?" she asked in her baby voice turning around so he could see her most prized possession. She looked over her shoulder to see Tedrick nodding his head up and down. She smiled.

"Take off my shoes." She ordered, and he slid her small pretty feet out of the heels. "Take off your clothes," she instructed next, which he did in three seconds flat and climbed back in the bed.

Blu'Jai stepped her petite body up on Tedrick's muscular chest, balancing herself with her hands on the huge headboard. She arched her foot and ran her toes across his lips before he opened his mouth to allow her toes entrance.

"Good boy! I didn't even have to tell you to open up!" she said as he sucked her toes. "I like that." she stared at him intensely. Blu'Jai was in control so she was in her element, in her zone.

She slid her wet foot out of his mouth and massaged his thrill drill with it.

"Tedrick, do you think you know me well enough to get married?" she asked, continuing to play with his love muscle with her foot.

"I love you Blu, baby. Yeah! I know you well enough," he smiled.

"Do you think I want my titties sucked right now?" she asked.

"Yes, you do!" he grinned. She was turning him the fuck on.

Tedrick pulled her breasts out of her dress and licked them tenderly. He ran his tongue around her nipples and squeezed them soft with his big strong hands.

"What do you think mommy wants now?" she asked in a whinny voice.

"You want me to taste you." Tedrick had gotten very good at that, by the way.

"Veeery good!" She purred in her baby voice. Real incremental progress has been made!

She grabbed his long monstrous dick. She licked her full lips with her mind set on giving him a world class blow job, and that's what she did. Her head bobbed up and down on his dick and she could feel Tedrick pulling her dress over her ass. He lifted her up and turned her around so that her ass could greet his face. Over their months together, Blu'Jai became a junkie for having her ass in someone's face, and had taught him how to give her head like a porn star, and now he was extraordinarily talented with his tongue. He had gotten so good that they rarely ever did sixty-nine because she would always lose her concentration and get lost in what he was doing, leaving her to have to finish him off after he was done. She was so proud of herself for teaching a young man how to be such a thorough lover.

Tedrick was putting it down and as usual Blu'Jai's focus went to being tasted.

"Ummmm baby, you're eating this ass!" she moaned as she spread her cheeks with both hands so he could go deep.

She bounced up and down in pure bliss, grabbing the top of his head with an arch in her back, sitting straight up and went to town working her pussy as Tedrick lapped her nectar.

"Ohhhhhh!!!" She screamed, as she started raising her ass all the way up off his face and crashing it back down with speed and force.

The sound of the loud slaps her ass made each time it collided with his face had her in ecstasy.

"Oh my God! Oh! Mmm, eat this shit! Aww!!! Fuck yeah!! Hell Yeah!!" she screamed before Tedrick slapped her on the ass.

"Suck this dick," he ordered and smacked her ass again as he continued to lick her into a frenzy.

She was still holding her butt cheeks open for him, so she swooped his dick in her mouth with no hands. She sucked on his balls with his dick lying across her face, then struggled to get his shaft back into her mouth. She was light-headed and got lost in the rhythm and Tedrick's moans, wrapping both hands around the base of his dick in search of his happy juice. She sucked her jaws in, making it look like she had huge dimples, trying to suck a stubborn orgasm out of his body.

"Cum for me daddy!" Blu'Jai sang as she got up and positioned herself on all fours so he could take her from behind.

Tedrick slid his dick in, smacked her ass and grabbed her hips. He slammed into her backside causing it to jiggle uncontrollably.

"Wait daddy!" Blu'Jai moaned, but Tedrick wasn't trying to hear it. He began to bang that ass even harder.

"Wait daddy! Don't…don't…don't stop…Fuck that feels good!"

They switched positions, and she put her legs on his shoulders. She bent one knee and Tedrick held it up by the back of her thigh.

"That's it, daddy! Get your nut! Get it daddy, get that nut!" Blu'Jai moaned as Tedrick worked her pussy.

"Fuck this pussy baby. Fuck me just like that!" she felt him explode inside of her and she came with him.

"I love you baby!" she said and thinking to herself that it was an unexplainable and marvelous feeling. She squeezed and milked his dick with her vaginal walls.

"Damn that was good." She whispered. "I can't believe that I'm going to be getting fucked like this for the rest of my life."

"So, is that a yes?" he asked excitedly hugging Blu'Jai.

"Yes, baby. Yes, I'll marry you!" she said with her head laid on his chest.

CHAPTER 12

Never tell me the odds.

Blu'Jai threw a graduation, engagement and going away party all in one, on Tedrick's graduation night. Everyone congratulated them, and Tedrick wished all his old teammates luck as they prepared to go off to play ball at colleges across the nation. Blu'Jai had on an all-white pantsuit, and Tedrick was dressed in all white too. While standing around mingling with everybody, Blu'Jai showed off her big diamond rock, and she received plenty of compliments.

  Tedrick and Blu'Jai waited a couple of weeks and they went to the courthouse to get married. This was only a temporary fix though, because they planned on having another wedding later down the road when he got his NFL contract. Days later they moved to Austin, which was about three hours from Dallas. The townhouse Blu'Jai had gotten them was in a very nice area. It wasn't far from the school campus, which was good because of all the late practices and late hours Tedrick had to spend in the weight room on campus for summer season training. She knew if they had moved further away that it would be an inconvenience for him.

Tedrick quickly built a close relationship with the star wide receiver for Texas and often brought him home with him for dinner, which Blu'Jai always made sure was plentiful and delicious. His name was Rosco Brown and he was a Sophomore from Sacramento, California. At six-foot-seven-inches tall, blazing speed and sure hands, he was a very touted NFL prospect. Rosco and Tedrick spent a lot of time together and practiced a lot on their own, trying to develop chemistry. They both knew that the more success they had practicing with each other the better chances they had to make it to the next level.

Summer training was over, football season started and Tedrick had won the starting Quarterback position. His hard work had paid off, and he led the Longhorns to a victory in his first game. He threw four touchdowns and ran for one in the blowout defeat against LSU. After winning his first college victory, the team was going to have an after party and Tedrick was eager to go.

Tedrick was getting dressed when Blu'Jai walked in the bedroom holding Kyler.

Blu eyed his tight-fitting Texas T-shirt and how it showd off his bulging arms and chest. "Don't forget you're married." Blu'Jai said sucking her teeth as she bounced Kyler on her hip.

"Blu chill out! Damn I'm just going to hang out with the guys tonight to celebrate, but I won't be gone long." Tedrick was looking in the mirror, still prepping himself and admiring how well-toned he was.

"Yeah! What the fuck ever!" she said storming out of the bedroom. "Don't get down here and start showing out nigga, because I've got some showing out in me too!"

"What's bugging you?" he said slipping on his leather jacket.

"Man, I have Kyler all day every day and I don't say shit! Hell! I want to get out this motherfucker sometimes too!" Tedrick glanced over at Blu'Jai with a surprised look on his face.

"Look, I'll keep her tomorrow and you can go out or we can get a babysitter and go out together. Okay?" he said, kissing her lips.

"You make me sick sometimes, but I love you. And you better not have your black ass out all night either! I ain't playing Tedrick!!!" Blu'Jai sulked.

Tedrick jumped into his Jaguar and headed to the party. He couldn't believe his eyes how live the place was when he arrived. There were bad bitches everywhere the eyes could see. Fraternities and sororities were repping their shit. The Omegas were stomping through the crowd and the Kappas were twirling their canes, dazzling the crowd.

"Heeeyyy!! Mah-man!!!" A guy screamed draping his arm around Tedrick's shoulders. "That was an unbelievable game!" the strange dude said handing him a cold Corona.

"Oh, I don't drink." Tedrick said holding up his hand.

"Bullshit!" the white guy screamed. "This is a party! Hey everyone, we got one that doesn't want to party!" he announced.

"Bring his ass here!" some more guys yelled.

Tedrick noticed that some of them were on the football team as the guy pulled him over to the group. They handed Tedrick a long tube and everyone gathered around him, females and all.

"Drink! Drink! Drink!" they all chanted.

Tedrick held a thumb high in the air and put the tube to his lips. Alcohol poured down his throat and he heard cheers like he had just scored a winning touchdown. Then something honey-colored and sexy, with a huge home-grown ass and supersized titties pulled him onto the dance floor. She grinded her ass against his crouch and gave him an instant erection. He was drunk by then, and before long, the same white guy that had gotten him drunk bounced over to him rocking to the beat.

"Hit this bud!" he said and handed him a weed bong. Tedrick was so drunk that he grabbed the bong and inhaled the weed smoke.

The inhalation of the smoke made him cough so hard that he thought his insides were about to come out.

"Let me see that thing!" a white young blonde with a slender but curved frame said. She took a hit and held the smoke in, then joined in the dance with Tedrick and the girl he was dancing with already. The white guy nodded with his approval and screamed, "Parrrrttttyyy!!! Party! Party! Party!!! Before bouncing off to pass the bong to someone else.

"Great game, Tedrick!" the blonde said, as she rocked side to side snapping her fingers.

"Yeah! Looks like we will be able to win a lot of games with someone as good as you playing for us!" the other girl commented.

"Thank y'all, but I better get out of here," Tedrick said looking at his watch.

"So early?" the blonde said in a disappointed voice. "I'm Amy and this is my roommate, Lisa. We were wondering if you wanted to come back to our place with us and, you know, have a little private celebration for the win."

"You won't regret it!" Lisa intervened.

Tedrick looked at his watch, "I wish I could, but I can't," he said and moved towards the door exit as they followed.

"Girlfriend?" Amy questioned.

"Wife," he said holding up his wedding band.

"What she don't know won't hurt," Lisa continued.

"Sorry guys. I hate to miss the party. It really sounds like fun, but

I'm going to have to pass." He said before heading outside to his Jag to go home.

Tedrick arrived home and Blu'Jai was up waiting.

After taking one look at him, she was pissed. "Yo ass drunk and I smell weed all over you!" Blu'Jai screamed. She turned off the lamp and snatched the covers over her head.

"Man chillout, I only had one drink," he slurred, turning the lamp back on. Blu'Jai snatched the covers from over her head and just stared at him.

"Tedrick you are riding around here fucked up and you know that all eyes are on you! Folks just waiting for you to fuck up! For you to be so smart, you sure can do some dumb shit sometimes!" she said.

"Yeah I know - like getting married!" he screamed.

"Oh yeah? That's how the fuck you feel?" she screamed back.

"Man, you always bitching about everything and I get tired of this shit!"

"You can kiss my ass. My whole ass, nigga! I'm your fuckin' wife, and when you fuck up your daughter and I must suffer! But fuck you Tedrick! I can't believe you said some foul shit like that!" Blu'Jai couldn't stop the tears from falling from my eyes.

"Blu' I didn't mean that," he said sitting on the side of her bed and putting his arm around his wife.

"Damn! That's some fucked up shit to say!" she cried and buried her head in his chest.

"I know, and I'm sorry. I didn't mean it. You and Kyler are the best thing that ever happened to me," he said as she continued to lay on his on his chest and sob.

"You think I'm always bitching?" she asked.

"Well you…well yeah, I do," he said, honestly.

"Tedrick, I have to protect you. Protect us! I'm 29 years old and you're 19. We've been together for nearly 2 years and from day one I've always been like a mother to you as well as a lover." she said.

"You're right and I apologize," Tedrick said sincerely.

Blu'Jai couldn't help her controlling nature. Calling the shots and running the shit was just a major turn on for her.

"We don't have any problems baby. We cool," he assured her.

"I love you Tedrick." she said in her assuring baby voice.

"I love you too! Now I'm tired, so let's get some sleep."

Tedrick didn't wait for her to respond, he left Blu'Jai sitting on the bed and headed towards the bathroom. He took a quick shower, then came out and jumped into bed with his wife,. But sleep didn't come anytime soon. Blu'Jai slipped his dick out his Polo boxers and put it in her warm mouth. Make up sex for them was always the best, and tonight was no exception to the rule. Blu'Jai put Tedrick to sleep after he busted two good nuts, but she laid on her side of the bed thinking.

I'm not about to let him fuck this up for us. I don't give shit how he feels about my bitching. If I can keep his head straight, we'll be rich in the next year or two! I'm not about to go back to having to steal clothes and shit! Fuck that! She grabbed her cell and walked into the bathroom. She locked the door and sat on the toilet, scrolling through her call log and dialed a number.

"Hello." A husky voice answered.

"You sleep?" she questioned in a whisper.

"I was, but what's up? Blu'Jai had no conscience or remorse. She chalked it up as everyone had skulls and bones in their motherfuckin' closet. Even though she married Tedrick, she still had no problem doing her dirt.

"I was just kind of missing you," she cooed with a giggle.

"It's only been a couple of hours since I've seen you!" Rosco chuckled. "I thought ya boy would be home by now," he questioned.

"He is, but he's asleep. Can you believe he came home drunk and high?" she shook her head in disgust.

"High?" Rosco asked surprised. "Man, they piss test too much to be getting high." he stated.

"I got right on his ass! Believe me!" Blu'Jai sucked her teeth.

"Like I got in yours tonight?" he boasted arrogantly.

"Well not that much." she laughed. "You play way too much!" she giggled. "But I let him know he was fucking up," she said seriously.

"Well you better get off the phone before he wakes up." Rosco warned. "I don't want to have to kick his ass over his bitch."

"Right!" Blu'Jai said as she smiled. :Boy, you crazy...but I'll hit you later."

"All right."

"Are you coming over tomorrow?" she asked, almost a pleading voice.

"Prolly! Your boy wanted to study and go over some plays with me before we play Baylor." he replied.

"Okay good! What do you want me to fix you for dinner?" She perked up at the thought of seeing Rosco again.

"Let's try tacos!" He smacked his lips together.

"Tacos it is, then. Maybe you can find a way to get rid of Tedrick and you can have me for dessert," she teased and giggled.

"I'll work on it." Rosco promised. Rosco usually didn't fuck with scandalous ass females like Blu'Jai, but her freaky ass was one he simply couldn't resist.

Blu'Jai deleted Rosco's number and flushed the toilet. She felt fucked up about what she was doing because she loved Tedrick and she didn't want to hurt him. But Rosco was an insurance policy. He was going Pro and when she noticed the way he would watch her whenever Tedrick wasn't looking, she saw Rosco as a backup plan in case Tedrick didn't make it.

One day Rosco showed up at their townhouse when he knew Tedrick was in class. Blu'Jai started not to open the door but he was looking fine as hell in his Polo outfit so she opened it. She knew she didn't have no damn business opening that door the way she was dressed but she honestly enjoyed the attention she always got from men, especially Tedrick's friends.

"I was just in the area and decided to stop by," Rosco smiled.

Blu'Jai seemed distant, but only for a second. "Want some juice or anything?" she asked, smiling from ear to ear.

"Yeah, juice would be cool. Where is Kyler?" he asked looking around.

"Oh her bad ass asleep, thank God." she said.

Walking to the kitchen, she could feel his eyes on her ass, and her red booty shirts crawling up her crack. She made her ass clap while she walked. It was a slow, lewd, sexy walk. She heard Rosco whisper, and she giggled to herself. She smacked her lips and thought, *'I'm a bad bitch!'*

As she opened the refrigerator and bent over to find the juice, she suddenly felt a finger slide beneath the cloth of her small shorts and pull them out the crack of her ass.

"Damn they were all up in there." Rosco said as Blu'Jai turned around and asked him what the hell he was doing.

She didn't know how to react because she didn't know if he was like a gossiping ass female or kept his mouth shut.

"Just helping you get that shit out of yo ass."

She playfully punched him on chest. She didn't know why, but her pussy had gotten wet.

"I'm serious Blu, that ass fat as hell. I would stay in there too if I could! Them shorts lucky as hell!" Rosco laughed, then stuck the finger he had just dug in her ass, in his mouth.

"You're so full of shit." She smiled and fanned him off. "Freaky ass..." she shook her head from side to side. "How does it taste?" She teased.

"Like cotton candy. I'm for real! These young ass bitches don't have anything on you! Tedrick is a lucky man!" he said, wishing that he could have some of Blu'Jai.

"Yo young ass probably wouldn't even know what to do with my ass if you could have it. This ain't what you want, bae. You probably a one and done nigga." Blu'Jai flirted.

"Why don't you try me?" Rosco challenged as Blu stepped in front of him and sat his bottle of juice on the table.

His big strong hands gripped her waist and spun her around. Rosco squeezed her juicy ass cheeks and spread them apart. He buried his face between them and released his grip, causing her cheeks to slap his cheeks.

"You serious?! You gotta be kidding me!" Blu'Jai grinded on his face for a minute before stepping away. Even through her shorts she could feel his tongue poking and prodding anxiously to get to her treasure.

Blu'Jai looked him in his eyes for a few seconds as she stood in front of him in silence. She wanted to see if he would back down from her stare, but he didn't. She picked up her cell phone and called Tedrick, never once breaking eye contact she had with Rosco.

"Do that again with your face."

Blu'Jai stared at Rosco a few more seconds before slowly turning her ass back around to feel his face buried in it.

"Hey baby! What's up?" She asked when Tedrick picked up his phone. Her voice was spunky.

She reached for the back of Rosco's head and just rubbed it like he was a good boy, and honestly in her mind he was.

"On my way to class, what's up?"

Pausing to take a breath., she raised one leg up slightly off the floor and pounded her monstrous ass against his face three times with force before turning back around to face him

"Just wanted to know if you wanted anything special for dinner, you coming home after class or to the weight room?"

Her gaze into Rosco's intensified. She reached for his dick to see if he was hard. She squeezed it through his shorts and was impressed with his size.

Damn, she mouthed with an ugly ass frown on her face.

"Me and Rosco gonna work out then I'll be home. I may bring him with me if it's good with you."

Rosco's dick was hard as hell. She slowly unzipped his fly and released his African artwork. She had to lay eyes on that thing. She looked at him and mouthed the words, *Damn, Daddy.*

He smiled proudly as she stroked it a few times. Rosco could read her lips loud and clear.

"That's fine. He can cooome," Blu'Jai sang slowly.

She went and locked the front door then came back into the kitchen and leaned over the table on her elbows. She arched her back, locked her legs at the knees and looked over her shoulder with her ass in the air.

"You talk a good game now let's see you back it up." She said. "I like it nasty. So, let's see what that head is like, then I want you to take that big dick and blow my back out."

Rosco pulled up a chair and peeled her shorts down to her thighs. He buried his face in her pussy, then stood up behind her and pounded Blu'Jai from behind relentlessly, with a tight grip on her waist and thunderous pumps into her sweet warmth. They fucked until Tedrick's class was over, then Rosco met him at the gym. That evening at dinner, Blu'Jai kept having flashbacks as they all sat at the table. Tedrick's friend has just finished fucking his wife only a few hours ago, in the same spot Tedrick was eating.

They had been fucking every so often, since that episode. Blu'Jai wasn't trying to spoil Rosco. She just wanted to secure her a spot just in case. She climbed back in bed, kissed her husband on the back of his neck, snuggled up behind him then fell into a deep sleep.

CHAPTER 13

The question is not who you can see yourself being with, it's who you can see yourself being without.

Blu'Jai didn't realize that playing college football required so much travel. Most of the time she only attended the home games, but she was thrilled to have the opportunity to meet so many famous NFL stars. Tedrick and Rosco attracted attention from many of the players who'd had their positions previously, and knew that while trying to build their careers in playing football, there would be many more people to see and meet.

Blu'Jai had something interesting going on the side that could make money for her as well. She managed to accumulate an impressive list of contacts from the guys who often offered to finance a "how to book" on the art of giving head, if she'd write it. They promised to buy their wives and girlfriends the book, because she could teach them a thing or two. She was propositioned for reality TV shows about football player wives, but she was too afraid of her dirty laundry to be aired, to accept.

As for life with Tedrick and Blu'Jai, it continued to progress. Tedrick led Texas to the Rose Bowl in his first season, which they won, and an after party was thrown afterwards. Tedrick had started hanging out at the after parties after every game. He had just pledged the Omega Psi Phi fraternity, and the Q-Dawgs were known to be a wild bunch. He had picked up the alcohol habit and would come home drunk maybe twice a week.

Blu'Jai tolerated the shit since he usually got drunk at home anyway. She would just go to sleep. If he was one of those stupid ass niggas that like to clown when they get a little liquor in their system, she would just shut his ass down. She didn't feel like using the energy that it would take to fight that fight and win, so she just let it go.

Before going to the after party, Tedrick stopped by the carwash to rinse off his Jag. He was a star on campus, so everybody showed him mad love the second he stepped through the door.

A woman handed him a cold bottle of Bud beer and he took a big swallow then started bobbing his head.

"Hey!" the girl screamed, handing him another beer.

Rosco quickly made his way over to Tedrick, and they did their signature handshake, then gave him a brotherly hug.

"Bunch of bad bitches in the building!" Rosco grinned at his quarterback while eyeballing the scene.

Barks from his frat brothers came from everywhere and Tedrick threw his hands in the air Omega style and barked like a pit bull.

"Hey you," a soft, voice came from behind with a tap on the shoulder. Rosco smiled, admiring the female that had just tapped Tedrick. She was cute as fuck and thick as molasses.

Tedrick turned around and couldn't believe his eyes. She was by far one of the baddest females he'd seen in his life.

"Ayanna! What are you doing here?" he asked with a huge smile on his face. She was just as beautiful as ever and she was now super thick in all the right places.

"I was told you'd probably be here tonight! I went to the game today with some friends and I told them that it would be nice to see you again. I wasn't going to come, but they talked me into it. You looked good out there in the field today," she playfully punched his chest.

"Damn," she poked his pecks, admiring the hardness. "I see your butt is stepping up on the workout!"

"Had to get my weight up. You know I play with the big boys now! Man, I can't fuckin' believe this!" he said, reaching down to pick her up off her feet with a big hug.

"Boy you better put me down!" she laughed. "With your big self! I hear you done got married and things. I don't need your wife in here trying to clown me!"

"She at home with Kyler," Tedrick said.

"Wow, I bet your daughter's getting big!" Ayanna tried to laugh off everything that she felt.

"Yeah, check this out!" he said pulling out his phone to show her a picture of his baby girl.

"Ummm she sure looks just like her daddy, with her cute self," Ayanna said, honestly. She added, "I always knew you'd be a good father."

"Thank you," he beamed. He couldn't take his eyes off Ayanna.

"Look at you!" she said, playfully punching his arm. "You all big and buff now!" she laughed, squeezing his bicep as he made a muscle for her.

"Damn!" she smiled. "It's really good to see you," she sang. She couldn't help but touch his body. It had really matured.

"Hey, let's go outside so we can chill in my car, so we can talk in private." Tedrick suggested. Old times, old memories flooded his mind. He really missed this girl.

"You sure that'll be okay, because I don't wanna get you in trouble," Ayanna said with a concerned look on her face.

"Talking ain't never hurt nobody, Ayanna!" she noticed that he had a little too much to drink by the way his words slurred, but he was an adult now, so a few drinks were socially acceptable.

Tedrick grabbed two more beers out the barrel that was filled with the ice and bottles galore. Ayanna followed him to his Jag. He had to admit the girl was looking downright gorgeous. She had on a pair of tight, denim jeans and top just as tight, and some high heel tan suede peep-toe zipper booties, that came to her knees. Her heels *click clacked* on the concrete with the rhythm of a prize winner stallion. Her arms were folded across her chest tightly and that caused her ass to sway a little from side to side, from left to right, as she walked to the car. Tedrick opened the passenger door then climbed into the driver seat and popped open his bottles of beers. "Care for one?" he offered her a bottle.

Ayanna shot him a stupid look, knowing he knew better.

"So, what's up girl?" he asked as he turn the heat on in the car.

The windows were tinted, preventing anyone for being able to see in or them able to see out.

"Nothing much," she said dropping her arms, revealing her huge rack. She noticed how wide his eyes were.

"What?" She questioned, with her eyes squinted. She was looking sexy as hell.

"I don't remember your titties being so big!" Tedrick licked his lips like he could just taste those honey melons in his mouth.

"Well that's because you were busy sweating Blu'Jai's titties," Ayanna popped.

"You tripping, 'Yanna," Tedrick stared at her. "It wasn't even like that," he assured.

"Well what was it like, Tedrick? You didn't even take the time out to say I'm sorry or goodbye. After all the years you and I spent together. That shit really hurt. I mean you're the only guy I loved. The only boyfriend I've ever had. And it was all taken away from me. For two years, I've been trying to figure out what I did wrong. Man…you fucked up my self-esteem had me thinking I was too fat, not good enough. I had a very rough patch in life and I really had to turn to God to pull through.

"You didn't do anything," he said, looking away from her stare. Her words pierced his soul. The shit was hard to hear.

"No look at me," she said using her index finger to turn his head back around by his chin. She held his chin with her index finger and thumb. They stared at each other silently for a few moments, but their hearts were screaming.

"It's been two years that I waited to have this conversation. The least you can do is look at me." She had a serious look on her face.

"See we were both young when I met my wife and shit just went fast. I mean I had no intention of hurting you. It's just we don't have control over some shit."

Before she knew it, she had slapped him! She tried to slap the bullshit that he was saying right out of his mouth.

"Like who you stick your dick in! I know that you had to play some part in this since we weren't having sex. I just don't understand guys! They want a woman that's not in the streets disrespecting herself, but when they get one, they always end up screwing around with some hoe. I'm not trying to disrespect your wife, but it is what it is."

Tedrick rubbed his face but her words stung much harder than the slap. "Ima keep it real with you. Yeah, sex had a little to do with it, but it wasn't just that. My wife is really a good woman and she treats me right."

"Oh? And I didn't? Ayanna frowned. "I didn't treat you right Tedrick?" She pointed to her chest. "I treated you like a freaking king!"

"I'm not saying that you didn't," Tedrick said.

"I was saving myself for you Tedrick. I could have accepted it better if you would have said Ayanna I really want to have sex. And you could have at least given me a chance to take it there or not, but you didn't. You just started fucking other people and left me."

She looked out the window. "Blu'Jai took my dreams and turned them into my nightmares."

"Well I'm sorry and I was wrong. That's really all I can say at this point," he said, taking another swallow of his beer.

"Thank you, your apology is accepted," she said sarcastically.

"Come on 'Yanna," Tedrick pushed her thigh playfully. "Cut a nigga a little slack, I'm trying to apologize."

She cracked a light smile then leaned over to kiss his cheek. "We're good." She allowed herself to calm down. What was done, was done and it was time to move on. "I better go before my friends put out an APB on me." Ayanna wiped a lone tear from her eye.

"Wait a second, he said pulling her face back to his with two fingers under her chin. He licked her lips and they tasted like candy apples.

She opened her mouth to allow his tongue more access. He reached around her to cup one of her ass cheeks to pull her over to his body. He cupped one of her huge breasts and she moaned as her tongue danced inside his mouth. She was back in familiar territory and it felt good. Ayanna's mind was racing as she stepped one leg over the arm rest and positioned herself between his legs. They were both breathing heavy as she sucked and licked on Tedrick's neck.

"You gave my pussy away yet?" he asked, rubbing her crouch.

"Umm-hmm," she moaned as she fed her breast to him. Suddenly a light flashed through the driver's side window. The glaring light was followed by the three hard taps.

"Police! Step out with your hands up where I can see them," one of the two officers said with a hand on the pistol.

"Uh...hi, officers what's the problem?" Tedrick asked, stepping out the car with his hands up.

"Hey! That's Tedrick Moss!" One of the officers said excitedly.

"Yes sir, I'm starting quarterback for Texas." he stated as a matter of fact.

"I know who you are, and I don't give a shit to be honest about it! The other officer spat. "You could be the quarterback for Jesus and the 12 disciples for all I care; it doesn't make me none!"

Ayanna made herself decent and climbed out of the car. Since she was going to law school, she figured it be best if she handled the situation.

"Hi! I'm Ayanna Cole and I'm a law student at Texas Southern University. What seems to be the problem?"

"Other than you indecently exposed and being minors in possession of alcohol?" the first officer asked.

"Whose vehicle is this?" the second officer asked.

"It's mines, sir." Tedrick stated.

"Well it looks it's going to be a long night for you *big shot,* because I'm going to have to arrest you," the officer smirked.

"What the fuck for!" he shouted.

Tedrick thought like hell. He couldn't be getting arrested! It would-be all over ESPN by morning, and that shit would spell big trouble for his football career.

"Officer, this must be some type of mix up. Why is he going to jail?" Ayanna questioned.

"I advise you to shut up, Miss Law School, unless you want to take the trip with him," he snapped and started snapping the cold steel handcuffs around Tedrick's wrists. "I'm starting to feel like my life is in danger!" he raised his hand on his holstered pistol and eyed her.

"I advise you to watch how you're talking to me officer because I do know my civil rights and I will slap a civil suit on you so fast you won't know what hit you! Now, I'm going to try this to again: what are you arresting him for?" she said with her hands on her hips.

The officers weren't sure how serious Ayanna was, so they decided to back up and act professional.

"Ma'am this car was reported stolen months ago, so he is going down for auto theft and a minor in possession of alcohol."

"That sounds more like unauthorized use of a motor vehicle, I mean he has the keys and I can verify that he's had the car for over a year so I don't see how you can charge him with anything."

"That's for the judge to decide," he said, putting Tedrick in the back seat of the police car.

"Do you need me to come and get you out?" Ayanna asked.

"Nah! Thanks though. Imma call my wife to come and get me, to straighten this out. She knows where this car came from," he said as they close the door and pulled away.

CHAPTER 14

The struggle you're in today is developing the strength you need for tomorrow.

Tedrick made his phone call from jail. Blu'Jai angrily waited until the automated recorded voice finished, then she accepted the call and immediately lit into Tedrick's ass.

"You've got to be fuckin' kidding me, right? I mean you can't be fucking serious, Tedrick!" Blu'Jai screamed into the phone receiver. "You have a lot of nerve calling here asking me to come get you. Nigga I wish I would!"

"You my got damn wife! Who the hell else am I posed to call?" He screamed back.

"Try your bitch Ayanna!" Blu'Jai yelled.

"Look, I'll explain that after you come and get me! I'm sitting in a jail cell and you want to bitch about some shit like that? This isn't the time for that Blu. Just get up and come get me out of here," he pleaded.

"Hold your breath!" Blu'Jai said. "Hold your muthafuckin' breath."

"Bitch!!! Fuck you!!!" Tedrick shouted before slamming his phone down.

Blu'Jai knew her husband was heated, but hell so was she. He had his motherfucking nerve to call her after he had been cupcaking with a bitch in his car all night. And not just any bitch; it had to be fat ass Ayanna.

"You here?" she said returning to the call she had on hold.

"Yea I'm here," Rosco piped in.

"Sorry about that. That was Tedrick." She sighed.

"Where is he?" Rosco asked nosily.

"Still in jail, where do you think?" her voice cracked.

"I didn't know if he had gotten out. So, what's he talking about?" Rosco inquired.

"He's talking about, come get him!" Blu'Jai answered as she stretched out in the bed and pulled the warm covers over her body.

"What you gone to do?" He continued to ask her.

"Rosco, you just told me that my husband was in a parked car, windows fogged up, his ex-girlfriend all on top of him with his shirt off. What the fuck do you expect me to do?" she screamed clearly upset about the whole situation.

"I'm just saying, if the school finds out about this, it could be trouble, and all the talk about him winning a Heisman Trophy will be out the window," Rosco said, hoping to change her mind about getting him out of jail. He really didn't want Tedrick to fuck off his career, plus he needed him for at least another year, to raise his stock in the NFL draft. A receiver is only as good as the guy throwing him the ball, and Tedrick made the game easy for Rosco, with the perfect touch spin and accuracy of each pass.

"Didn't you tell me you bought that Jaguar for him anyway? So how is he being charged with theft?" Rosco asked in a concerning tone.

"I didn't say I bought that car for him!" Blu'Jai said agitated.

"You did. You told me you bought it for him his senior year of high school." He knew she had told him that without a doubt, because he felt like that was some real shit for a woman to do.

"No, I said I gave him the car," she said, rolling her neck.

"Well if you gave him the car, how is it stolen?" Rosco asked.

"Actually, a guy I used to deal with left the car to me when he went the prison. Either he's out and reported the car stolen or one of his people did it, I don't know!" she said, now frustrated.

"So, you got your husband riding around in another nigga car and they reported it stolen! That's fucked up Blu! Does he know all of this?" Rosco asked in a worried tone.

"No! He doesn't! He's not going to know either!" She spat, getting tired of Rosco acting like he was a saint.

"He won't hear it from me. But I think you need to go and get him." Rosco didn't approve of the shit Blu'Jai had done. He couldn't believe it and was hella disappointed. He knew Blu'Jai was trifling but her antics never cease to amaze him.

"Did I ask you that? Huh!!! Look I've got to go. I'll talk to you later," she said, not bothering to wait on a response from him, before she ended the call out of frustration.

Blu'Jai laid in the bed and replayed her conversation with Rosco, mainly about Tedrick not winning the Heisman trophy and being in trouble with the school. She reluctantly pulled herself out of bed and threw on some sweats and slipped her hair back into a ponytail. She walked into Kyler's bedroom to get her together and thought to herself, *I can't let my heart override my brain. I better go get his stupid ass before it gets worse than it already is, so off to the jail house.* She and Kyler went to pick up Tedrick.

"Tedrick Moss! Let's go, you made bail!" the officer screamed from the cell door. Tedrick pulled himself up off the concrete bench, happy to be headed back to his life of freedom. He was handed back his belongings, then escorted to the waiting area. All the anger he had in his heart not even an hour ago seemed to have vanished into thin air.

Unthinkable questions hung between them as they stared at each other in complete silence. A half smile curved Ayanna's mouth as she stood back on her bowed legs with her arms folded tightly across her chest.

"Hi," Ayanna said, in a low but high-pitched voice. Tedrick took her luminance makeup-free skin, as she moistened her lips with a swipe of her tongue.

"I wasn't expecting you." Tedrick finally spoke.

"Surprise," she smiled. Tedrick wrapped his arms around her, and she had no choice but to hug him tight. He inhaled a fragrance she was wearing and became instantly intoxicated.

"Thank you for coming to get me. I didn't know how I was going to get out of here." He looked at her and realize how much he truly missed her, not only as a partner, but more so as a friend. She always batted a thousand in that department. Always.

"Boy you know I would never leave you hanging. I kept calling down there to see if you were out, and they kept telling me no. So I said to myself, *I know that I wouldn't want to be sitting in jail,* and I took it upon myself to come and get you. I didn't want to run into your wife, but I said if I did, oh well; she'll just have to understand that we've been friends our whole lives, and real friends make sure that each other are okay," Ayanna said with a sincere tone.

"You don't have to worry about running into her." Tedrick's temperature boiled just thinking about the shit Blu'Jai had pulled.

"Why? What happened?" She asked as he slipped his arm around her waist and they walked out the jail and headed to her car.

"Somebody told her about us being in the car together last night and she went crazy. She refused to come get me, so I appreciate this more than you know he said.

"It's no problem, big head," she laughed. Ayanna drove Tedrick home and he couldn't keep his eyes off her the whole trip.

"You still remember my number? Or did you forget it?" Ayanna asked as they pulled into his townhouse.

"Yea if it's the same. Why?" He asked.

"Use it sometimes, you don't have to be a stranger. You know we go too far back." She said, turning her head to look out the window.

She wanted to avoid eye contact because she was still hurting inside from him leaving her, and she didn't want Tedrick to see the tears that were cascading down her cheeks.

"I'll call you." He paused and sighed deeply. "Let me know how much I owe you and I'll get it back to you," Tedrick told her.

"Don't worry about it. The money doesn't mean anything to me." She dismissed his comment with a fan of her hand. "I'm just glad that I was able to help." She finally looked at him. They stared at each other briefly before Tedrick climbed out of the car and waved at Ayanna as he walked to his front door. She waved back by holding up her index finger, wiggling it up and down then drove away.

Tedrick unlocked the door and walked into the house to find Blu'Jai and Kyler dressed to go.

"How you get out?" she asked. Tedrick didn't even bother to answer her question as he brushed past her and went into the living room and sat on the couch.

Blu'Jai came in there right behind him so, he got up and walked back out with Blu'Jai hot on his heels. He just went to the bedroom and laid across the bed.

"Do you hear me talking to you Tedrick?" she screamed, without even pausing to give him a chance to say anything. "Who the fuck got you outta jail and how did you get home??"

"Why? My motherfucking wife wouldn't come get me!" he said in a dismissive tone. he couldn't believe that she was even coming at him with this foolery after she'd left him sitting in a damn jail cell.

"So what, you got your hoe to come get you?" she worked her neck with her hand on her hips. She was ready to start a war up in that camp because Tedrick had her *all the way fucked up.*

"Someone who gave a fuck came to get me!" he said, getting off the bed walking to the bathroom, closing the door in her face.

"Oh! Now I don't give a damn?" she screamed banging on the door.

"Open this goddamn door, Tedrick!" Blu'Jai shouted. She was furious. She rammed her shoulder into the door like she seen in the movies to try and break it down, but the damn door didn't bulge and she damn near knocked her shoulder out of its socket.

"Leave me alone. I'm about to take a shower and go to bed. I'm tired. My wife left me in jail all night!" he said.

"I better not find out that Bitch Ayanna got you out! I swear Tedrick, I'm going to kill you! I'm going to kick your black ass, just let me find out!" she spat.

Tedrick climbed into the shower and tuned out all the bullshit Blu'Jai was saying. With the water on extra hot, he closed his eyes and thought about Ayanna and how much he missed her. He loved Blu'Jai but at times he questioned their relationship.

Stepping out the tub, he lifted the toilet to take a piss. Once he was finished, he flushed the toilet, but it was backed up. Tedrick grabbed the plunger that was sitting on the side of the bowl and pushed it into the water. He pumped a few times, then pulled the plunger out. His eyes squinted at what he saw floating in the water, because he couldn't believe what the fuck he was looking at.

Tedrick slowly reached into the toilet and pulled out a piece of condom wrapper, and two used condoms. Never once had he ever used a condom with his wife, so what the hell was his bedroom toilet doing stopped up with them?

"Blu'Jai!!!" He screamed to the top of his lungs as he snatched the bathroom door open. "What the fuck is this?" He yelled, holding the condoms to her face.

"I don't know!" she defensively said. "Where you get that?" She looked puzzled.

"Out the gotdamn toilet! Who you been fuckin'?" Tedrick asked her.

After denying it over and over, Blu'Jai finally broke down and told him that she had sex with someone out of anger to get back at him for being with Ayanna. Since she wouldn't tell him with who, Tedrick threatened to have the DNA extracted just to see who was fucking his wife. Hearing this Blu'Jai panicked.

"I was upset about Ayanna and I fucked up! I was just upset! We both were wrong, but at least now you know how it feels so we can move on and get stronger."

"Bitch get yo shit and get the fuck out my house!" Tedrick scolded.

"What?" She asked in a surprising manner.

Tedrick proceeded to tell her to get the fuck out his house because he didn't want to hurt her. Being one to never back down, Blu'Jai dared him to touch her. Tedrick grabbed her around the neck and began choking her down before she even knew what happened.

Gasping for air, Blu'Jai reached up and dug her fingernails deep into his face clawing his ass like Freddy freaking Krueger.

"Bitch imma kill you!" Tedrick spat with venom, then smashed the condoms into her mouth.

She tried to bite his fingers off, so he grabbed a fist of her hair and shook her head like a wild dog! She screamed. He growled. They both cried.

Still trying to stuff the condoms down her throat, they fought tooth and nail in that bedroom. Blu'Jai knocked over lamps and was even able to grab a vase to throw at him.

Suddenly there was a knock at the door, and Tedrick turned her loose.

"This aint over, bitch!" he said. Then he slapped her so hard the condoms flew out of her mouth. "Stay right there, bitch!" he warmed with a point of his finger as she laid on the floor crying.

Tedrick walked-to the door to see two police officers standing outside.

"Can I help you?" he asked through the door.

"Can you open the door please? It's the police," a voice said from behind the door. Tedrick opened the door and the officer continued.

After chatting with the officers and letting them know that everything was fine, they were about to leave when Blu'Jai came storming out of the room attempting to leave. When she saw the officers, she turned on the water works.

The officers then stepped into the home and saw the damage. After speaking with Blu'Jai they determined that they had to take Tedrick to jail.

On the way to the station, Tedrick had a long talk with one of the officers and he appreciated the advice he gave him. After being processed in, he was finally able to make his phone call.

That phone call was to Ayanna, of course.

CHAPTER 15

She loved him. He loved her. But it wasn't that simple.

Ayanna didn't ask no questions when she heard that Tedrick had been arrested again; she simply came and got him. He really appreciated Ayanna for everything. Her being there for him had him thinking that just maybe he had made the wrong choice.

"I appreciate you coming through for me like this again," Tedrick said as she drove with her focused on the dark highway with both hands on the wheel. "I don't know what came over me, I feel like I had an out of body experience and I just lost it," Tedrick said.

"Tedrick I love you, you know I do. But I think you should be having this conversation with your wife. I don't want to sit here and pass judgment on anyone. I know if you were my husband, I'd want you to talk to me about our problems not some other woman," Ayanna said as she drove him home.

On the drive home, both he and Ayanna had a heart to heart about her feelings and whatnot. When he got closer to his house, he took Ayanna's phone and called his wife.

"Hello," Blu'Jai answered on the first ring.

"I'm on my way home. Don't go to sleep because we need to talk." Tedrick implied.

"Who got you out?" She questioned.

"We will talk about it when I get there," he said.

That sent Blu'Jai in a frenzy. She began to scream and yell but Tedrick ended the call just as quickly as it started. Him hanging up in Blu'Jai face prompted her to call Ayanna's phone back over and over again.

After realizing he was not gonna pick up, she sent a nasty text message to Ayanna's phone.

"I told you that I better not find out that your hoe got you out of jail! Don't worry about talking when you get home cuz I won't be here nigga! You and your hoe can have fun."

Ayanna suggested that she come in and talk to Blu'Jai face to face, but to their surprise, Blu'Jai had taken off and left Kyler home alone.

CHAPTER 16

The thing about smart motherfuckers is … they sound like crazy motherfuckers to dumb motherfuckers.

Blu'Jai headed straight to Rosco's. When she asked him if she could stay there, he was more than happy to have her in his apartment.

The next morning, Blu'Jai woke up to an empty apartment since Rosco was gone to the gym. He texted her to see if she wanted breakfast and she told him that she did. Rosco was stopping at McDonald's, so Blu'Jai asked for a sausage, egg and cheese biscuit, hash browns, and a latte. She sent the text, then snugged back under Rosco's covers.

Not even ten minutes later, the front door slammed and Blu'Jai thought it was Rosco making it back already, but it wasn't. She opened her eyes to two masked men standing over her.

She wanted to scream for help, but she was afraid to.

The men asked for money, but she told them that she had none. Since they couldn't get money, they decided to have a field day with her body.

Jerking the sheet off Blu'Jai's body and slinging it to the floor, one of the masked men grabbed her by her ankles and pulled her across the bed. Once he had her pinned down, he told her how he heard she had some good pussy. Shocked, she now realized that they were going to rape her.

In the midst of getting raped - or so she thought - she realized that it was Rosco and his roommate. Rosco invited his friend in after telling him how good Blu'Jai's pussy was. The rape scene came from him telling how Blu'Jai liked to role play.

After Blu'Jai's first threesome, Rosco and Blu'Jai started talking about his football career. She told him how she accepted money for Tedrick to play ball at Texas, and she even tried to get him on board. And just like always, Blu'Jai got her wish. She was going to set up a meeting with an NFL scout for Rosco.

Within three days, Blu'Jai made a million-dollar deal, found a new condo, and was even having new furniture delivered. She couldn't believe her good fortune. Although she did miss Tedrick and Kyler and the life that she had with them, she was happy to be free of motherly duties. Blu'Jai made a plan to get Rosco; she just had to put it in affect.

The threesome he forced on her just didn't sit well with her. She didn't give a damn about how much she liked it; no one called shots of which dicks went in her pussy but her. She didn't feel bad at all that she made the anonymous phone call to the athletic director tip them off about the agent she'd hired for Rosco. She had no plans on him going back to school. She wanted him to enter the draft that year, but he said he wasn't ready. She had seen him make unbelievable catches repeatedly, so in her eyes he was ready as ever. Blu'Jai didn't have time for Tedrick's shit. She was ready to sip champagne in the VIP sections of the clubs with more important people than athletes. She was ready to hang out with folks like Michelle Obama and Kim Kardashian, because those type of women had their shit together.

CHAPTER 17

Why do my fights for the things I want always have to be the hardest?

Tedrick was trying to grasp the fact that Blu'Jai had left him and Kyler high and dry. He and Ayanna had started spending a lot of time catching up. They both had found each other's company therapeutic. Tedrick hadn't spoken to Blu'Jai in three days, which was fine with him. He loved his wife, but infidelity was something he didn't think he could forgive. Hundreds of women had pranced around in front of him multiple times. He had resisted the temptation for the sake of his marriage, but his wife couldn't do the same.

Weeks passed, followed by months, and the distance between him and Blu'Jai grew further and further apart. She had finally texted him, but they hadn't seen each other face-to-face since she left. After he told her about his indefinite suspension from the team, she asked for a divorce.

Blu'Jai was watching ESPN faithfully when she heard all the talk about Tedrick's character issues: his team suspension, his scholarship being in jeopardy, and the fact that the NFL frowned on guys that had a troubled history. She knew without a doubt that the Plan B would be a decision she had to make.

"I can't believe a kid with so much promise and talent could be such a bonehead!" the ESPN analysts were saying. "No way can you put all your eggs in one basket with this guy. I don't see anyone taking a chance on giving him millions to lead their ball club, when he's clearly a liability. That's probably why he didn't win the Heisman!"

Blu'Jai asking for a divorce finally was what really opened Tedrick's eyes that she was only using him. Ayanna knew this was true, but she didn't want to rub it in his face by saying I told you so.

"I think you need to talk face to face and resolve this instead of trying to talk about it over the phone." Ayanna suggested. "I'll keep Kyler until you get back if you need me to," she said, rubbing the tip of her fingers down the spine of his back.

"Thank you, Yanna," he said. He began to wonder how he even ended up with a woman like Blu'Jai when Ayanna had been there the whole time. "I mean that. Thanks for everything," Tedrick whispered, then pressed his lips against her cheeks.

"Umm..." she mumbled, turning her head to meet his gaze, then kissing his lips softly. They sat and stared each other in the eyes for what seemed to be an eternity, both revealing what their mouths wouldn't. Their eyes told the story of their bond. Their love. Their history.

Ayanna stood up and walked out of the bedroom to check on Kyler. She was busy trying to sing along with Sesame Street Muppets about the letter 'A.' Ayanna kissed her on the head, then felt her stomach muscles tighten as she went back into the bedroom and closed the door behind her. Tedrick ended a short conversation he was having on the phone when he noticed her reenter the room.

"That was Blu'Jai, I told her we needed to talk face to face and she agreed. I guess I'll go back to Austin today, but I'll be back tomorrow."

Ayanna loved Tedrick and was willing to stand by him no matter what and through whatever. She thought that maybe she had stuck her foot in her mouth by telling him to meet with Blu'Jai, but if anything was ever going to become of her and Tedrick again, she was going to be sure that Blu'Jai was out of his system. Her mind was racing 100 miles an hour, but she threw caution out the window. She pulled the Dolce and Gabbana shirt over her head, revealing her honeydew melon size breasts.

Silence hung in the air between them as his eyes fell on her swollen breasts. She unzipped her tight pants and pulled them halfway down her round ass.

"I want to do it," she said she moistened in her lips with a swipe of her tongue.

"You sure? I mean you know I'm mar-" he couldn't get his words out.

"Unhappy, "she cut him off. "You're not married; you're unhappy."

Ayanna caressed the side of his face with her fingertips. "I've always dreamed of you being my first everything. You're my first love and I want you to be my first lover." Ayanna had no doubt that this was the aman she wanted to give one of her most precious gifts to. She wanted Tedrick to introduce her to real womanhood.

"Unhook my bra, "she said, walking between his legs turning her back to him. He quickly let her titties free then tossed her Bra to the side.

He grabbed the sides of her jeans and finished pulling them down. Tedrick kissed the small of her back while she slowly slid her thick ass out of her panties. Her sexuality was insatiable as she carefully undressed him, and they fell into each other's arms. Tedrick wanted Ayanna's first experience to be special. So, he used everything he had: mouth, lips, body and even his soul. He shared his words with her to make her gasp in pleasure and bringing her to an ultimate orgasm. They started in the missionary but explored several more before Kyler 's cries were heard on the baby monitor.

The lovemaking session was dissolved into breathless giggles as Ayanna grabbed her robe then went to see about Kyler.

Tedrick got in the shower, then got dressed. He walked into the kitchen and sat down at the table next to Kyler.

"Do you want one of these? "Ayanna asked, holding up a knife with peanut butter on it.

"Yeah, sure," he said, kissing Kyler.

Ayanna sat a sandwich in front of Tedrick, then folded her arms across her chest.

"So…what do you think? "she asked nervously.

"It was well worth the wait, but I'd like to try it again, when baby girl's not around," he smiled and looked at Kyler.

"Really? So, you like it?" Ayanna asked excitedly.

"Yeah! Why wouldn't I?" he smiled. "I wouldn't trade it for nothing."

"Well I'm not as experienced as you know who," she teased.

"It was good, bae," he assured.

After chatting with Ayanna for a little while longer, it was finally time for Tedrick to hit the highway so he could go back to Austin. Gathering his things, he asked Ayanna if she was sure that she was going to be okay with looking after Kyler. Ayanna assured him that they would be fine.

Tedrick climbed into Ayanna Nissan Maxima and headed to Austin. He felt funny driving a woman's car and not having his own, but right now a car was the least of his problems. He was blessed to rekindle the friendship he had with Ayanna. She really had been coming through for him in more ways than one. She had talked to one of her lawyer friends and he'd agreed to take all of Tedrick's pending cases. Plus, he still loved her. He'd never stopped. Ayanna was the only person that didn't try to pass judgment on him. Even his mom was disgusted with him, with all the missteps he had taken.

. After a 3-hour drive, Tedrick found himself at home. He noticed that all of Blu'Jai clothes were gone and reality sunk in. He grabbed a bottle of water from the refrigerator and turned on the TV. After watching a few minutes of ESPN, he flipped the channel.

He was tired of hearing the sports reporters talk about how much of a disappointment he was. He settled back into the sofa and watched a poineless reality TV show.

Suddenly, he heard a key slide into the lock on the front door. It was rainy and the storm clouds were dark. Blu'Jai didn't have an umbrella with her, so when she rushed in, she was dripping puddles of water onto the floor. She had on a pair of Fashio Nova jeans that the water had stuck to her frame like Reynolds Wrap. Her long hair was wet and stringy curls hung wildly over her face and down her back. She took a second and pulled her hair behind her ears.

"Hi, "Blu'Jai said, smiling weakly.

"Hey, "Tedrick responded.

He really missed his wife and her flawless beauty. He was starting to second-guess his desire to grant her the divorce that she had asked for. He wondered if it was possible for them to get past their problems.

He got up and grabbed a bath towel from the linen closet. "Here, dry yourself off," he said, offering the towel to her. She didn't take the towel. Blu'Jai just continued to ring the front of her shirt out on the rug without a word been said. Tedrick wrapped the towel around his wife and pulled her into his arms, only she didn't return the affectionate gesture he had made. He was crushed.

"Tedrick, we need to talk," she whispered, then took a deep breath.

"That's what we're here for, right?" he said and sat back down on the couch. "Blu'Jai, I'm not sure that I want to give up on us," he admitted.

"There is no *us* anymore, Tedrick. You disrespected me and screwed your life all up. I need stability in my life, and you are far from stable now,"she said, sitting, on the love seat.

"What about Kyler? She needs her mother. And I was kind of thinking we could at least talk about working things out. I noticed that you haven't even asked about your daughter," he said, wondering why she was being so unconcerned.

"I know she's okay. You can have her. I'm sure you'll find a good replacement mother that will help you take care of her. As far as us working out, I may as well be truthful with you. I'm dating someone else and I'm moving on with my life."

"What the fuck you mean you're dating someone else? Bitch! You still wearing my ring!" Tedrick was heartbroken and furious at the same time.

"Just what the fuck I said! I found someone who's a better fit for me, and I figured you were mature enough to except and respect that!" She stared a hole through Tedrick.

Suddenly, they both heard the sound of a car horn blow twice. "Look I've got to go, okay." Blu'Jai said, standing up. "Take care of yourself and Kyler. Tell her I love her."

"Bitch! You don't love nobody but yourself! I hate I didn't listen to my mama! "He said disgustedly.

"Right! Would've saved us both some trouble!" she said, as the horn blew again. "Like I said, I've got to go, but my lawyer will be in touch with you soon." she said, heading out the front door.

"Who is that? "he asked.

"My business! "She spat.

"No, bitch! It's my business! I know you didn't bring no nigga to my house!" he screamed.

"You brought your hoe over here! So, what's the difference? "She stepped back, snatching the door open to leave. Tedrick couldn't believe his eyes when he saw who was sitting in the driver seat of his wife's Infiniti, and he ran outside behind Blu'Jai.

"Oh, this is the perfect fit. You're talking about! Rosco!" He screamd at the top of his lungs. He was hurt that a guy that he felt was a friend, would betray him that way. "I can't believe this shit!" he said, and big faced her to the cold wet ground.

Tears errupted from his eyes as he watched the raindrops beat down on his wife's body. Tedrick stormed back into the house as Rosco climbed out of the car to help Blu'Jai. He wrapped his arm around her waist and opened the passenger door for her to climb in. But before he could close the door, he felt the burn of hot metal piercing his flesh. He crumbled to the concrete as shots continue to ring out.

Pop, pop, pop, pop!!! Tedrick was standing in the doorway with a smoking pistol, the same pistol that Blu'Jai pulled on her ex Miles.

"Why the fuck did you do that?" Blu'Jai screamed, hysterically jumping out of the car to help Rosco.

Tedrick looked at her with nothing but hatred in his eyes, as he walked back to his house and shut the door behind him. He looked at the big picture of them over the fireplace and shot a hole into Blu'Jai's face as he sobbbed. He heard police sirens in the distance and walked to the bedroom. He grabbed the box of bullets from the top shelf in the closet and loaded the 22. He had no plans of going to jail. As he sat on the edge of the bed, he ran his hands across his with face and sniffled.

"FREEZE!!!" Tedrick suddenly heard several officers scream from the doorway with their weapons drawn down on him. "Don't!!!"They shouted as he raised a gun to his head. "Don't do it, son! "They pleaded.

"My life is over, "he cried.

"It's never as bad as you think it is kid!"

Tedrick pressed the gun to the side of his temple, then looked into the officers' eyes.

"I didn't deserve this shit, "he said, crying uncontrollably. "She's my wife," he whispered. "My motherfucking wife! "Tedrick screamed to the high heavens.

"PUT! IT! DOWN! "An Officer warned again.

"Can't do that," Tedrick sobbed "Tell my mother I'm sorry… "

"Tedrick!!! Listen to me son! "an officer pleaded. "You're a thinker, a smart man. This is not the answer. Think about your daughter. Don't leave her in this cold world without a father. You pull that trigger, it will be a mistake you can't ever reverse. "

"Tell my mother and Ayanna and my daughter that I love them," he said, then squeezed the trigger.

CHAPTER 18

Still gone shine in the storm…

"Mane, did you see that catch?" Hood screamed, as Rosco caught a 60-yard pass, putting the Washington team up by ten.

"Mane that Rosco is a bad motherfucker! I'm gonna win the bet I made, right?" Hood teased, laughing and nodding his head.

"Yeah probably so," Tedrick agreed as they sat in the day room of the jail watching the Washington and Houston game.

"Tedrick Moss! You have a visit!" the CO screamed. He quickly went to his cell and changed into his tight whites that were starched down, and slipped on his Rhino boots.

Visitation was important to inmates. It was the only real connection to happy days in the life they once knew. Jail was a place where months and sometimes years could pass without one person taking the time out of their lives to come and see someone and show them that someone in this world loves them.

As Tedrick walked through the hallway in route to his visit, inmates of all ages and races plastered smiles across their faces and told him to enjoy his visit. Visitation to a prisoner was like Christmas to a kid.

He walked into the visitation room and was greeted by Ayanna and Kyler.

"Daddy!!!" Kyler screamed happily when she saw her dad.

"How's daddy sugar pop? "He hugged her tight and spun his daughter around.

"I miss you daddy!"

These were the days that reminded him that life was still worth living by the presence of love. Ayanna was quietly watching their father and daughter moment and the sight of it was worth every second of the two-and-a-half-hour trip that she had to drive to see him.

Once Tedrick put Kyler down, Ayanna seductively pushed away from the table and stood up to get her hug. Tedrick squeezes her ass cheeks and kissed her tenderly. "Damn you smell good," he whispered in her ear.

"So, do you, "Ayanna smiled, rubbing her hand over Tedrick's rock solid chest. "Your mama told me to tell you that she'll be down here next weekend and she loves you. "Ayanna mentioned.

"Bet, "he said, taking a seat at the visitors table.

"I got you a couple of sodas, chips and cookies.

"Thanks! "He said popping open a soda can.

"So, how are you?" Ayanna asked.

"I'm good! Just watching the game. Rosco just got a touchdown!" Tedrick said, hanging his head.

"Bae, don't worry about him. God has just another plan for you. That's all," she said sympathetically.

"What? A prison jail cell? "he asked sarcastically.

"I don't know. But I do know He's got his hands on and around you, Tedrick. How else can you explain still being here on this earth? He didn't allow you to remember to put a bullet in the barrel of that gun when you were trying to squeeze the trigger and end it all. He didn't let Rosco die knowing that a murder charge on top of the other charges would've handed you a life sentence."

"You're right. But it's hard to sit in here while *she's* out there living it up. I saw her on TV all hugged up with him in an interview on ESPN the other day. She don't even try to communicate with Kyler."

"Three years, Tedrick, and it's all over. Don't get in any trouble and we may be able to get you home sooner." Ayanna reached across the table and held Tedrick's hands.

"Yeah. I know it's not that long, compared to the time I could've gotten, and that some of the rest of these guys have to do. I'm thankful that your friend was able to get me that deal!"

"I am too," She smiled and leaned over the table to kiss him.

"Eww !!!"Kyler scrunched her little face up. Tedrick snatched her up and kissed her all over her face.

"I love you daddy! "Kyler smiled with joy and hugged her daddy tight around his neck.

"I love you too pumpkin, "he said. "I can't wait to get home to yall."

"We can't wait either baby! "Ayanna added. "Positive thoughts," she poked his chest. "No more of that negative mess. We can't be unappreciative of the blessings God has given us and then turn around and ask for more."

Tedrick felt good after his visit. He laid in the back of his cell, thinking about Blu'Jai and Rosco. After he got shot, the school declared him ineligible to play. And after receiving benefits of cash and gifts, he was kicked off the team, so he entered the draft. There was a lot of concern about his durability after the shooting. Some of the bullets couldn't be removed. But he still went to Washington in the third round of the NFL Draft. He received a nice contract but was nowhere near what it could've been without the injuries he had endured.

"What's crackin, cuz? How was your visit?" Hood asked as he walked into the cell.

"The Fam is good man! My daughter is getting big as hell. Who won the game? "Tedrick asked.

"Mane! Hoe ass Rosco fucked off my money! He dropped the pass in the end zone! You should've killed that nigga!" Hood laughed.

"Nah. I'm glad I didn't, it aint worth it! Plus, I'm not trying to stay up in here forever," Tedrick said shaking his head.

"Shit me neither, cuz! My brother-in-law got me a bad ass lawyer and he say we got them on my appeal," he said with confidence.

"I hope shit works out for you, homie," Tedrick said.

"It will. Say, what you gonna do when you get out? "Hood questioned as he walked to the door to check for the corrections officers, then pulled a joint out of his sock. "Want to blow this with me?"

"Nah, I'm good homie," Tedrick declined. "I don't know what I'm going to do when I get out. I know I'm going to stay with 'Yanna. She's real man, and she's been holding me down since day one. She even keeps my daughter and take care of her like she's her own. I respect that."

Hood inhaled the smoke and noded his head in agreement. "I'll probably see if my girl can find someone to hook me up with a job." Tedrick said.

"I'm a fuck with my brother-in-law, Blessed, when I get out, and we go do our thing," Hood said.

CHAPTER 19

People make mistakes; that's why pencils have an eraser.

Tedrick didn't have to do the whole three years. He made parole after doing just two years. Ayanna threw him a "welcome home" barbecue that a lot of his former high school teammates came to. Even Coach Griffin showed up. He wasn't coaching anymore, but all the kids he ever coached were like sons to him.

Tedrick was glad to be home with a chance to start a new life. Ayanna had just finished law school and was ready for Tedrick and her to start their lives as husband and wife. He paroled and was released to her place since she had moved back to Dallas, and they made love day and night. He was the man of her dreams. He always had been, and she was blessed that God had brought him back to her.

$ $ $ $ $

It was Sunday morning and they had just finished a passionate session of lovemaking, and now it was time for church. Tedrick kissed

Ayanna's belly, which was swollen to the size of a butterball. She was six months pregnant and glowing all over. Tedrick got up and fixed breakfast for his girls and Kyler was always happy when her daddy cooked breakfast. She knew he would always make her favorite: pancakes with lots of syrup and bacon.

After they ate breakfast, they got dressed in their Sunday's best and headed to Friendship West Baptist Church. The pastor gave a powerful sermon about ways of the heart.

Referring to God, Pastor exclaimed, "love yourself and love your brothers and sisters! You must love them to love Me."

After church service, they went to eat dinner at Tedrick's mother's house. Regina knew how to throw down in the kitchen. She made greens, roast, mashed potatoes, corn on the cob, a pound cake and stirred up some Kool-Aid to wash it all down. They all ate while they watched the Dallas Cowboys game. The Dallas Cowboys and the New York Giants was always a good game to watch. Tedrick enjoyed watching Dak Prescott operate. He had dreamed of being in his position one day, but all that went out the window, so he would just have to settle for working for Amazon.

Ayanna had come through for him again and got him a job. She made good money, but Tedrick was the type that always wanted to help bring something to the table.

On the first drive of the game, Dak was marching the Cowboys down the field with ease. He had them in the red zone and they were about to score with four passes, but he took a shot from a linebacker that broke his collarbone in the first three minutes of the game. After losing Dak, the Giants gave the Cowboys an old fashion ass whooping. The game was over, so they said their goodbyes to Tedrick's mom and left for home.

Monday morning had rolled around before Tedrick knew it. He pulled himself out of bed to go to work. He slipped on his jeans, some steel-toed boots and an old button-down shirt. He grabbed his Longhorn ball cap and slapped it on his head, then he headed to work after kissing Ayanna and Kyler goodbye.

His day at work was going so-so, but his stomach was growling, and lunchtime wasn't coming fast enough. Working at Amazon was pretty physical labor, but Tedrick didn't mind, because it helped to keep him in shape. He wiped sweat from his forhead with his shirt sleeve and tossed another box when the lunch bell rang. He raced to the vending machine and pressed D-2 after dropping quarters in the coin slot. A beef and cheese sandwich fell down the shoot and he quickly tore the package open. He had a text from Ayanna:

Call me on your break.

"What's good babe?"

"Coach Griffin called this morning looking for you. I gave him your cell number and told him you'd be off work at four," Ayanna told him.

"What did he want?" Tedrick asked.

"I don't know. He just said he really needed to talk to you, but he didn't have your new number."

He only had a few minutes left on his lunch break, so he decided to give the coach a call.

"Were you watching the game yesterday? I know you were! "Coach said excitedly.

"Which one?" Tedrick quizzed.

"The Cowboys game!" Coach answered and added, "Be honest."

"Yeah! You know I was mad they loss. I know you're not calling me to rub it in!" Tedrick laughed, remembering how much Coach Griffin hated the Cowboys. Coach was originally from New Orleans so he was a huge Saints fan.

"No, not at all! In fact, a buddy of mine called me last night and we started talking about Dak going down. You know they say that he will be out for the rest of the season."

"No! I didn't know that." Tedrick said, glancing at his watch again.

Coach was long-winded, and his lunch break was about over. Suddenly Tedrick regretted calling him before he had gotten off work.

"Yeah man! But anyway, we were talking and your name came up. He wanted to know if I thought you still had something left in your tank, and I told him hell yeah!" Coach shouted. "He knows some coaches for the Cowboys, and they want you to come and try out for them! This may be your shot, son! What do you think?" he questioned.

"When do they want me to try out? "Tedrick asked excitedly.

"Tomorrow! Can you get off work?"

"Hell yeah! I'll be there! Where do I go?" Tedrick was overwhelmed with joy.

"Be at Cowboy Stadium at seven in the morning. I'll meet you up there."

"It's a bet, coach!" Tedrick screamed. He couldn't wait to tell Ayanna the good news, so he took a sick day for the second half of his shift. He rushed home. As soon as he walked in the door, he picked Kyler up and carried her into the bedroom where Ayanna was changing the sheets on the bed.

"Baby! I have some good news! I talked to Coach and he told me they wanted me to try out for the Cowboys in the morning!"

"Are you serious? Babe, I'm so happy for you!" Ayanna shouted and hugged him tight.

"I just hope I can impress the coaches! I mean I'm not in the best of shape anymore," Tedrick admitted.

"What did I tell you? God has a plan for you. He keeps opening doors! Just keep your faith in Him and things will work out fine, "she said.

"You stuck with me even when I didn't deserve it. I love and appreciate you for that." Tedrick kissed Ayanna's forehead and looked into her beautiful eyes.

"I did just what I was supposed to do and I will stand by the one I love," Ayanna laid her head on Tedrick's chest.

CHAPTER 20

You have a greatness within you!

Despite being away from the game for damn near three years, Tedrick still hadn't lost a step. He amazed the coaches with his footwork, ability to elude tackles, and could toss the ball 50 yards down the field effortlessly. He called Ayanna after tryouts was over. An hour later, he was sitting in Cowboys owner Jerry Jones' office. Coach had called a sports agent to come in and read over the contract. After seeing the contract looked good and in tact, Tedrick signed his name to a $1 million deal, and he was officially a Dallas Cowboy within 24 hours. To think that he was doing back-breaking warehouse work yesterday, and today day he was a millionaire, was unbelievable to him.

For the next month, he worked out to condition his body, and learned the playbook. Then it was finally game time for Tedrick. The buzz around town about the former high school and Lonestar standout making his debut for America's team had the crowd in a frenzy. The Cowboys hadn't won a game since Dak went down and Tedrick was getting his first NFL start against Washington. Ayanna and Kyler were at the game, both wearing number 2 jerseys with "Moss" on the back. Tedrick's mom Regina, and Coach Griffin was there too.

The crowd erupted as Tedrick took the field for the first time as a Cowboy. He had a jittery feeling in his stomach, but wouldn't allow himself to get flustered. He was animated as he ran out on the field to his teammates, then lined them up.

Tedrick executed with extraordinary efficiency. He dominated every aspect of the game with his distinguished style of play. By halftime, the score was Dallas 21 and Washington 3. Tedrick didn't know how he would feel about seeing Rosco again, but surprisingly he didn't feel anything. Rosco had emerged as Washington's number one receiver, although his contract wasn't the number one receiver type money. He had openly criticized the organization and expressed his displeasure and the team's treatment of him.

The second half of the game started and Tedrick continued to dazzle the crowd, closing out the game with the Cowboys 35 to 10. Dallas had a great defense, which was stingy and hard-hitting. They were so hard-hitting, they broke Rosco's leg.

The year went on and Tedrick only got better with each game. Although they didn't make the playoffs, the Cowboys were sure that they had found their quarterback. They signed him to a $60 million deal during the offseason and every sports reporter had changed their tune.

"I knew he was destined for greatness!"

"He's a future Hall of Famer!" they all said. The news of his contract was a hot topic, as everyone expected Dallas to make a strong run at the Super Bowl with Tedrick under center.

Washington decided to cut Rosco, which he didn't take too kindly. He threatened the head coach and the police even had to escort him out of the Redskins' facility. Rosco ended up being sued and no one wanted to take a chance on him and his reckless behavior. Word was, that the Cowboys was looking at Rosco, but passed on him considering the history of him and Tedrick.

Tedrick bought a huge house in Arlington, and on March 7, Ayanna gave birth to a bouncing baby boy and named him Cedrick.

"I'm ready to get married!" Ayanna said as she gazed into little Cedrick's eyes.

"As soon as this divorce is final, you'll be Mrs. Tedrick Moss. Blu'Jai keeps rescheduling the court date, but she has to show up next month."

"I'm just ready for that woman to be out of our lives for good," Ayanna said, taking a deep breath and closing her eyes trying to imagine their forever.

"I know baby, I am too! "Tedrick assured.

$ $ $ $ $

Tedrick quickly put on his custom fitted Hugo boss suit and a pair of Polo dress shoes. Today was the big day. He had to be a divorce court at 8 AM and it was already 7:15.

"Come on yall if you're coming, or I'm going to leave you!" He yelled at Ayanna and Kyler.

"I'm coming, I just need to put on Cedrick's shoes," Ayanna replied from the bedroom.

She had on an Armani skirt and jacket suit with a pair of Fendi heels that gave her attire a classy yet sexy look. They all piled into his new Tesla truck and headed downtown to the Dallas courthouse. Traffic was light on the freeway, which was unusual for a Monday morning.

Usually everyone is in a mad dash to get to the workplaces. Tedrick found a parking space with 15 minutes to spare. They walked into the courthouse and took the slow elevator up to the fourth floor. They found Judge Davis' courtroom and took a seat in the hall, waiting until eight.

"Baby, I'm going to take Kyler to the restroom," Ayanna said, then kissed Tedrick's forehead.

"Okay, but hurry up. It's almost 8," he said, setting his phone to silent.

"We will, you just watch the baby! "Ayanna grinned, happy the divorce date had finally come.

"I've got my little man," he said to Ayanna's back as they disappeared around the corner. Cedrick smiled and laughed, which bought joy to Tedrick's heart. "You're happy this about to be over too, huh? "

"Gosh, he is so cute! What's his name? "Tedrick heard the soft voice speak, causing him to look up.

There she stood in her money green Chanel pantsuit that hugged her hips and ass like a glove. She had on a pair of Christian Louboutin heels, Gucci shades covering her eyes and a Gucci bag draped over her arm. Blu'Jai was the booty queen and her most prized possession was on full display, causing Tedrick's eyes to gaze over. A smile spread across her face when she saw his eyes caressing her body.

"His name is Cedrick," Tedrick finally spoke.

"Oh that's cute, Tedrick and Cedrick!" she laughed her beautiful laugh.

"So where is Rosco? You didn't bring him?" he asked sarcastically.

"Rosco and I are through. He wasn't a good fit for me. Besides I'm a married woman." Blu'Jai said fanning off his remark.

"Trying to fix that," he stated quite frankly.

"Don't be ugly Tedrick. It's been over a year since we've seen each other. Be nice! You're looking good too boy and I'm proud of you! I've been watching your games and you know I'm still your biggest cheerleader," Blu'Jai eyed him seductively.

Blu'Jai looked good as hell to him too but he wasn't there about to tell her.

"Oh! I didn't know you brought bobble head with you! "She said noticing a Ayanna returning with Kyler from the restroom. "I still can't believe you got tied back up with that little bitch," Blu'Jai continued.

"Hey darling! How was mom's baby? "Blu'Jai bent down and spread her arms wide open to greet her daughter, as Kyler started running in their direction.

Kyler stopped dead in her tracks, like she had been learning the moves watching her daddy play. She turned around and looked at Ayanna, who was approaching her quickly. Blu'Jai snatched the shades off her face.

"Kyler, come back to mommy," she waved to her daughter. Blu'Jai's smile was wide, but Kyler looked at Blu'Jai, then took off running full speed to Ayanna and held onto her legs for dear life.

"Pick me up, mommy!" she whined to Ayanna. Ayanna scooped her up in one motion, and Kyler buried her face in Ayanna's chest. Blu'Jai, somewhat embarrassed, slapped her shades back over her eyes and stood back up. She ran her fingers through her long weave and look back at Tedrick.

"I'm not signing those divorce papers," she said rudely. Ayanna shot her a menacing look and stood beside Tedrick.

"What do you mean you're not signing the papers? You've held us up long enough!" Tedrick spat with a frown on his face.

"I mean what I said! I'm not signing them! I don't want a divorce! I want my husband and daughter back," Blu'Jai confessed in her most sincere voice.

"No bitch! You don't have a husband or daughter anymore!" Ayanna screamed, losing her composure. She was sick and tired of Blu'Jai's antics and today she was ready to give her another beat down. "You're a classic anal-retentive bitch! A fucking half price hoe and nothing more, and I'm not going to stand here and let you pull this shit again! You forfeited your spot as a wife and mother, bitch," Ayanna cried.

"Tedrick can you please control your hood rat?" Blu'Jai asked in an icy and snobbish tone.

"Oh! I got your hood rat! You fake ass wannabe! "Ayanna spat, putting Kyler down.

"Oh, I got your hood rat! "Blu'Jai repeated, mimicking Ayanna's voice in a cruel fashion. I wish your fat ass would touch me; I'll have your ass under the jailhouse," Blu'Jai threatened.

"Look Tedrick! I love you and I know you love me! Yeah, I know I've made mistakes in this marriage, but I want us to be a family again," "Blu'Jai pleaded, ignoring Ayanna.

Tedrick had to admit to himself that he still loved his wife, but Ayanna was always there for him when no one else was.

Ayanna could be trusted, and he didn't want to give that up. The sight of Ayanna standing there in so much pain was too much for Tedrick to bare. He made his mind up right then and there. He walked over and hugged Blu'Jai tight. Blu'Jai gave a sinister smile while wrapping her arms around Tedrick, and Ayanna felt her stomach knot up. She could barely breathe or barely stand. The sight before her was just too much to handle so she took off in a mad dash. She had to get out of that building quick, fast, and in a hurry. Tedrick knew that in his heart Ayanna was his pick and she was his soulmate. He didn't want Blu'Jai or any other woman.

"I can't do this Blu'Jai. Our time is over. I love you and I wish you the best, but Ayanna is the one for me and always has been," he said.

"Watch the kids for me this one time, I've got to catch her," he asked, and took off down the stairwell before Blu'Jai could object.

"Ayanna!!!" he yelled, taking four steps at a time. "'Yanna baby, wait!" he screamed, trying to catch up with her.

When he made it to the ground floor, he spotted Ayanna leaving out the door. He continued to run behind her and finally got her attention when he made it outside.

"Ayanna! "He screamed at her, as she crossed the busy downtown street.

She turned around just in time to face her worst nightmare. Tedrick ran across the street with his eyes focused on Ayanna. Maybe that's why he didn't see the Range Rover until it was too late. The expensive SUV plowed into Tedrick, his body flew several feet, before landing hard on the pavement in the middle of downtown Dallas. The driver of the Range Rover quickly ended his conversation on his cell phone and climbed out of the SUV.

"Oh, God!" Ayanna screamed. "Someone call 9-1-1!"

The blaring wail of the ambulance siren filled the air as it sped down Commerce Street. The sound was one which let everyone know in proximity that God was busy. It was time for someone to be called home or either He was just in the business of handing out other blessings.

Tedrick grimaced in pain as the paramedics started attaching tubes all over his body. He could feel his own warm blood roll down his skin like beads of sweat. His whole body ached. He was weak from losing so much blood, but he had enough strength to say, "get the kids." Ayanna knew the kids were upstairs in the courthouse with Blu'Jai, because they weren't with him. So, she told him they would be fine, she was going to ride in the ambulance with him and she would call Blu'Jai when they arrived at the hospital. Suddenly he felt a sharp pain in his chest, a pain that felt like he was having a heart attack, and the ambulance loaded him up and off to Parkland Hospital they went. He thought he was somewhere between Heaven and Hell.

When the ambulance pulled into Parkland Hospital, news cameras were everywhere, doing live coverage of the new quarterback for the Dallas Cowboys being in a life-threatening car accident. People had questions, they wanted answers. The world wanted answers. But none could be afforded at that point.

Blu'Jai had received the news of the accident by receiving a phone call from Ayanna, so she brought Kyler and Cedrick to the hospital with her, dropped them off in a waiting room with Ayanna and left without saying anything. Ayanna paced the waiting room floor praying hard and heavy. She already called Regina, and she was on her way. Regina finally made it, and they were gathered in the waiting room. Ayanna needed a hug, so she bent down and picked up Kyler and hugged her tight. Kyler looked up at Ayanna's face and kissed her.

"He's gonna be all right mama. Daddy strong," Kyler spoke like a big person in a small body.

Kyler was smart! Really smart! Ayanna thanked God for her. She wished that she could have been as brave as Kyler was right then, but the fact was, she was scared. "I know baby. I know," Ayanna closed her eyes and nodded.

Thirty minutes later, a greying African American doctor walked into the waiting room. "Excuse me, Mrs. Moss? "He approached Ayanna.

"Yes? May I help you?" Blu'Jai had just popped up out of thin air.

"Excuse me?" Ayanna frowned. "What the fuck are you still doing here? "The look on Ayanna's face was that of pure disgust.

Regina sat in the waiting room, not saying anything. She was just sitting there being attentive to her grandkids and waiting on the status of her son's condition. Things had gotten a little overwhelming for her, with all that was going on: the feuding, the arguing, the whining, and the restlessness of her grandchildren. The situation that her son was in just made it feel as if her whole world was caving in, so she decided that she and the children needed a breather. She left the waiting room with her grandkids and they went to the chapel in the hospital to pray.

"If I didn't know any better, I'd think you were a retard! "Blu'Jai said. "My husband has just been in a serious accident and you have the audacity to question my presence? Actually, I'm wondering what *you* are doing here?"

"Ladies," the doctor started, "we have pressing matters at hand, so if you two will please put that stuff aside for a minute. I'd like to inform you on his condition."

"Okay. Sorry Doctor, how is he? "Ayanna asked nervously.

"It's really too soon to know for sure, but early indications are showing significant brain damage, from head trauma and a spinal cord injury. He's not breathing on his own right now and honestly there's not much optimism that he will make a full recovery at this point," the doctor informed them.

"So hypothetically, if he's able to pull through," Blu'Jai started, "he probably won't be able to walk with the spinal cord injury? So, are you saying it's also possible that he will have very little ability to communicate, if or when he does start to breathe on his own?" Blu'Jai inquired.

"Correct. So, I would like to ask if you'd like me to leave him on the breathing machine? Or if you would be more comfortable with allowing nature to run its course?" The doctor asked.

"No, go ahead and take him off the machine. That'll be fine," Blu'Jai advised, snatching her purse up to leave.

"I beg your fucking pardon? "Ayanna gave Blu'Jai the evil eye. "Continue with aiding his breathing doctor! Whether it's on the breathing machine or however! I need you to do everything that you can for him to improve his healing," Ayanna ordered, while never taking her eyes off Blu'Jai. *The nerve of this bitch,* she thought.

"I'm his wife! "Blu'Jai pointed to herself, then flashed her wedding ring. "I have power of attorney over this matter!"

"Estranged wife, *bitch*! I'm his fiancée and you two have been separated for years!" Ayanna shouted with frustration angrily.

"Is she still legally his wife? "The doctor asked.

"Yes, but this all happened while we were at the courthouse to finalize the pending divorce and-"

"He changed his mind!" Blu'Jai interrupted. "We decided to work on our marriage and that's when Miss Thang threw her little temper tantrum and ran away. Had she handled the situation like a grown ass woman and accepted the fact that Tedrick will forever be mine, we wouldn't be standing here right now."

"That's a damn lie!" Ayanna cried. "Shut up!"

"That's *my* husband! I called the shots in his regard. Always have, always will! Now doc, respect my wishes because I know my husband wouldn't want to live like this. And Miss Thang, you have 24 hours to remove your things as well as your new baby boy Cedrick's and Kyler's shit out of me and my husband's home." Blu'Jai laughed.

"Oh!! I get it! It's all about money! You want to see your own daughter out on the street?" Ayanna sobbed.

"24 hours! "Blu'Jai repeated.

Ayanna couldn't take it anymore. She tore into Blu'Jai's ass and beat her senseless. Within minutes, the police were on the scene, but not before Ayanna had ripped most of the weave from Blu'Jai's head.

"I want to press charges, officer!" Blu'Jai said.

"Please doctor! Don't listen to her!" Ayanna cried as she felt the cold steel being clamped around her wrists.

"I'm sorry ma'am, but I have a legal obligation here, hope you understand," the doctor said sorrowfully.

"Bitch! I'm going to kill you!" Ayanna promised, as she was being escorted away, like a woman deranged. "Please officer! You know who Tedrick is! Please don't let the doctors remove the breathing machine," she begged. As she lost the last bit of strength in her legs, two officers attempted to hold her up as she crumbled to the floor into a puddle of tears.

"I'm sorry ma'am but we have no control over that, we're sorry but we're going to need you to stand up and walk. It's not going to be that bad, you may only be charged with simple assault," he promised.

The doctor walked in Tedrick's room and bowed his head. He'd watch the kid grow up in the spotlight. He had a son around Tedrick's age as well. His heart was always filled with grief to see another brother laying in this position. After a brief conversation with God to take care of Tedrick's soul, he reached for the off button on the breathing machine.

"Don't touch that machine, doctor!"

An out of breath voice came sailing through the doorway. He turned to see to whom the voice belonged, and laid eyes on a beautiful woman. She rushed over to the doctor and grabbed his hand.

"I don't care about the orders you were given initially," she said.

"And you are?" the doctor asked, although the tears in her eyes told the story. He knew exactly who she was, and his heart smiled at the sight of her.

"Regina Moss, Tedrick's mother."

TO BE CONTINUED

Preview of *Selfish: Part 2:*

"Tedrick... you're barely climbing off your death bed and instead of thanking God for that; the first thing you do is call my shit on a fucken Saturday night about some divorce shit! Boy bye get off my phone. I'm not going to nobody's court and I've told you that I'm not signing shit but a check, good night!" She ended the call with the swipe of a finger.

As soon as Blu'Jai reached for the door the doorbell rang. She snatched it open with the quickness, "what!" She screamed agitated, shifting her weight to one leg. The bullshit was killing her vibe. "Good evening Miss Moss," he said, eying the Texas thoroughbred standing before him.

"Can I help you?" Blu'Jai's eyes squinted into Chinese like slits and she ogled the uniformed man at her door.

"I hate to disturb you like this but I have a warrant for your arrest and I'm afraid I'm gonna have to ask you to turn around and put your hands on the wall so I can frisk you..."

Made in the USA
Columbia, SC
28 May 2022